# Clues, Crushes, and

# Second Chances

### Lisa Buffaloe

*Clues, Crushes, and Second Chances*

Visit the author's website at https://lisabuffaloe.com.

Cover Design: JoAnn Durgin

ISBN: 978-1-957715-58-2 (eBook)
ISBN: 978-1-957715-59-9 (Paperback)
ISBN: 978-1-957715-60-5 (Hardcover)

# Clues, Crushes, and Second Chances

It all began with the murder of Aloysius P. Higginbotham, or at least, that's when Georgia Shaffer's passion for solving mysteries was born. Now a P.I. in the charming town of Garden Valley, Tennessee, she spends her days untangling small-town secrets, running background checks, and dodging unwanted advances at her family's outdoor shop. Mysteries Georgia could handle, but when it came to her heart, she didn't have a clue.

Clint Briscoe's goals for moving to Garden Valley after his ex-girlfriend's betrayal were to care for his grandfather, fix fences, manage the cattle, and guard his heart by avoiding women. Yet when a string of thefts brings an unexpected reunion with Georgia, the sparks fly faster than the bugs that seem to chase her everywhere. Clint's determined to keep his guard up, but Georgia's warmth and wit soon challenge his resolve.

As secrets and feelings collide, can two insecure and wounded hearts solve the biggest mystery of all to have the courage to take a second chance on love?


Quirky characters, a hefty dose of small-town charm, and a touch of mystery make *Clues, Crushes, and Second Chances* a clean romance full of faith, forgiveness, hope, and fun.

## *Table of Contents*

# *Chapter 1*

Georgia Shaffer never planned on being an investigator, not until Aloysius P. Higginbotham met a terrible end. Even as a six-year-old, Georgia knew her hamster had been murdered.

The prime suspect? The hawk that terrorized birds and small pets in their neighborhood.

Aloysius had been having fun in his hamster ball, enjoying being outside, running around the back patio, when it happened. The ball smacked against a rock, flinging Aloysius free.

Unfortunately, her hamster's freedom didn't last long. Georgia later found Aloysius's small, furry, lifeless body with telltale claw marks on his back.

Although she hadn't been able to save her hamster, from that point on, she was determined to help those she could.

Wildlife investigation was impossible as a career since her body was a walking buffet for every bug within a mile of her. After earning a degree in criminal justice, she joined her father's firm as a private investigator.

Well, at least she called it a firm. Her dad's business, Shaffer's Outfitters, located in a historic building on Garden Valley's main road, sold equipment for fishing, hiking, hunting, camping, and also provided private investigation services. Besides working at the outfitter's shop, Georgia spent most of her time doing background checks for companies.

Georgia sighed as she glanced out the second-floor window. In the bright sunshine of summer, a variety of shops, boutiques, antique stores, and new dining establishments surrounded the Courthouse Square. The town stayed busy, energized by the influx of new residents and curious tourists. Georgia sighed. Gone were the quiet days when she used to hang out at the old country store with her best friend at the soda fountain.

Two years ago, her small hometown experienced a growth spurt when SAU Tech chose Garden Valley as its base. The electronics company founded by Elijah Sausage wisely decided not to use his last name for the business.

Georgia moved to her chair and surveyed the photos on her desk. Her father, straightlaced and military-rigid, had married his exact opposite when he fell in love with her fun-loving mom.

A tap on the doorframe drew Georgia's attention. "Got a minute?" Her father, Richard Shaffer, a tall, lean, ex-military man, came into her office and sat across from her desk. "Tell me what you have on the Barbour case."

Even though she was twenty-five, Georgia straightened in her seat. "Yes, sir." She knew her father loved her, but still found his presence intimidating. "Jake's four-wheeler is still missing."

Richard's dark hazel eyes studied her for a moment. "It wasn't Melba?"

Georgia stifled her grin at the name of Jake's feisty older neighbor, Melba Marshall. "No, sir. Melba swears up and down she didn't take it this time." The woman had grown up in the mountainous area and was as tough as beef jerky, with more energy than most young people. Last year, Melba had "borrowed" Jake's four-by-four to run an errand when her car wasn't working.

"At least we can rule her out." Richard's eyes momentarily showed a spark of humor. "Let me know what the police say. I'll be downstairs. Don't forget you have the front desk after four today."

Georgia nodded. "I'll be there."

Her dad left her office, and her gaze swung to the photo of her best friend, Tanya Guthrie. Growing up on the same country road, they were known as the sleuthing sisters, solving mysteries such as missing pets and lost belongings.

On her cell phone, Georgia clicked Tanya's number.

Garden Valley's only police detective answered on the second ring. "I bet you're calling about Jake's four-wheeler," Tanya's voice laced with amusement. "Anything new on your end?"

Georgia shook her head as though her friend could see. "Nothing yet. I'm going to stop over at Jake's neighbors and check if anyone saw anything."

"I hope you find out something. The town's buzzing with rumors. Mr. Grady is blaming the theft on Bigfoot."

Georgia chuckled. "That's what he said when that motorcycle went missing last week. Maybe we should be searching for a big, hairy guy."

"Bigfoot or not, we've got to find out who the thief is. This is the fourth theft this month."

"We'll figure it out." The residents of their usually crime-free town were worried about the thefts. The strangest part was that SAU Tech employed most of the people whose equipment was taken.

"Are you working at the store this afternoon?" Tanya asked.

"Yeah, since it's Friday, we're open late. Mom and Dad are going out on their date night."

"You need to go on a date night."

"Yeah, right. Like that's going to happen." Georgia shoved a stray hair behind her ear. She hadn't been on a date in over a year. "You married the only cute, eligible bachelor in town."

"I did catch the best one. Blake is a dream. Sorry about

that." Tanya's last comment didn't contain one ounce of genuine remorse. Not that Georgia blamed her. Her friend deserved a good guy.

"You need to make yourself more available," Tanya continued. "There are plenty of men who visit or have moved to our town."

Georgia was ready for a change of subject. "We still on for a hike Saturday?"

"Definitely. I'll meet you at the trailhead at six thirty in the morning. See you then."

The call disconnected, and Georgia rose to her feet and stared again out the window. The new company had brought more people to the area, but many were married, and the few single guys she'd seen around town weren't her type.

Her criteria for a man might be a tad unrealistic, but why settle? The only guy she'd ever met who made her heart do that ridiculous flutter thing was when she was in high school. But he was two years older, had only been in the area when he visited his grandparents in the summer, and she hadn't seen him in years.

Maybe Tanya was right, and Georgia needed to make herself more available. It wasn't like she didn't get offers from some of the men who came into the outfitter store. Most of those were only visiting the area, and why would she want to date anyone who didn't want to live in Garden Valley?

Praying and waiting were her methods for finding a man. If she remained single, she'd ask God to help her be content being alone.

Georgia pulled her long hair into a ponytail and wound it into a bun. Or at least an attempt at one, since her hair was so thick it was hard to tame.

When she was younger, she always wore her hair down,

hiding behind the long strands, never daring to let the faint outline of her birthmark marring her face and neck be exposed to the world.

The fear of judgment and the ache of self-consciousness clung to her, making her shrink away from moments that might draw attention.

Now, though, each time she gathered her thick hair and pulled it up, she fought to be braver, to let go of the old embarrassment. She wasn't fearless, but she was trying to accept herself just a little more every day.

Sipping a cup of coffee, Clint Briscoe stepped out onto his grandparent's wide covered front porch and surveyed the green, rolling hills that now belonged to him. In the tree by the house, a bird chirped a cheerful tune. In the meadow, the black coats of the grazing cattle shimmered in the sunlight.

As a kid, Clint had spent most of his summers helping his grandparents on the farm. After his grandmother passed last year, his granddad suffered a heart attack, fell, and broke his hip. Even though he was sixty-eight and still in great shape, he wasn't able to care for the land and livestock, so Pops willed the farm to Clint.

It never occurred to him that he would inherit the property, given that he had two siblings. Thankfully, his triplet brothers had no interest in living in the country. His oldest brother, born a minute earlier, was a firefighter, and the middle brother, born thirty seconds later, now played professional football. Clint, born last, was the smallest of his brothers. He believed his siblings had taken all the resources in their mother's womb, leaving him at a disadvantage in terms of height.

The sound of running paws drew Clint's attention. Butch, the Great Pyrenees, and Dash, the Border Collie, hurried over and settled at Clint's feet, as if waiting for orders for the day.

"Hey, guys." Clint rubbed the tops of their furry heads. "We'll get going soon."

"Are you happy to be here?" His grandfather, Wayne Briscoe, stepped out of the house and, with a smile, approached him.

"Yeah, I am." After graduating from college in Texas, he lived in Nashville and worked long hours in the insurance industry. The money had been good, but nothing compared to the quiet of a morning in a valley surrounded by the Smoky Mountains.

"Don't miss the rat race?"

"Nope. Not a bit." Clint took a deep breath of fresh air. Being here allowed him to start over, free from the painful recollections of his failed relationship. His jaw clenched at the memory. He trusted the wrong friend and dated the wrong woman for way too long.

"Want to ride with me this morning while I check the fences?"

Clint glanced at his granddad, who still couldn't drive. "You mean, do you want me to chauffeur you so we can check the fences?"

"Yep," Wayne's blue eyes sparkled with mischief. "That's what I meant."

After gulping down the last of his coffee, Clint grinned. "Come on, Pops and pups. Let's ride."

# *Chapter 2*

With the sun barely peeking over the hills, Georgia stepped onto the front porch of her simple log cabin. Thankfully, when she got up early, the bugs didn't seem to bother her as much.

Savoring hot tea with honey, she settled into the old rocking chair. It still amazed her that her relatives had constructed the cabin in 1840. The horizontal logs had turned a dull gray from years of exposure, forming a stark contrast with the new, fresh chinking she had finished last month.

As long as the good Lord allowed, she'd make sure to take good care of the home that had been in her family for generations.

Georgia breathed deep of the mountain air. She loved living in the woods. As if acknowledging her thought, a bird whistled a cheerful melody, which another bird echoed. Looking through the trees, she could see the old white farmhouse belonging to her grandparents in the meadow.

At least she was close enough to check in on her grandmother since her grandfather had passed. Instead of Gramps, he'd been called Grumps, but even with his gruff exterior, the grouchy, cantankerous man had loved his wife and family well. Grandmother and Grumps had forty-five years together, and their love had been one for the romance books.

Grumps had been gone three years, and Georgia worried about her grandmother. Getting to her feet, Georgia moved to the front porch's simple railing made from rough-hewn logs. She didn't worry about her grandmother's health.

Georgia hated that her grandmother sometimes seemed lonely. Not that Janis Lucas would admit that fact. She still worked at Shaffer's with the rest of the family, remained active in the church, and even contributed to community activities. At sixty-seven, Janis Lucas was still in great shape and continued to turn the heads of men thirty years her junior. Georgia took a sip of her tea. In the last few months, Janis had seemed a little more chipper.

A muffled meow came from the right side of the porch. Captain Jack, the big one-eyed wildcat, proudly walked toward her, his tail stuck straight up as though waving a flag of victory.

Georgia took a breath to steady herself. The cat held a garter snake's tail in its mouth, while the rest of the still living reptile encircled Captain Jack's head, resembling Cleopatra's crown.

She hated snakes. Not that she was fond of the dead rats and mice the cat usually brought to her. "Thank you, Captain Jack. I appreciate the offering."

The big cat opened its mouth in a meow of acknowledgement, and in one swift motion, the snake uncoiled itself and slithered away into the forest. Captain Jack let out a startled yowl and gave chase.

With a shudder and a quick swig of the last of her tea, Georgia hurried inside to get ready for the hike with her friend.

After parking the teal 1965 Ford truck she'd inherited from her grandad, Georgia checked her backpack, making sure she had her water bottle, a snack, phone, and first aid kit. Having once been lost in the woods as a kid, she made sure to be prepared.

Several vehicles were parked in the lot, their passengers already gone. Surprised the trail was already busy, Georgia leaned against her truck to wait for her friend.

A gentle wind scented the air with a rich, earthy scent, mingled with the sweet tang of pine and the faint perfume of blooming rhododendrons.

Tanya's white SUV came to a stop two spaces away. She exited, slung her backpack over her shoulders, and headed towards Georgia. Her nose crinkled as though she sniffed something odd. "What is that smell?"

"I'm trying a new natural bug repellent. Witch hazel, lemongrass, and apple cider vinegar."

"I think you went a little heavy on the vinegar." Tanya waved her hand as though to clear the air. "No self-respecting bug or person would want to come within a mile of you."

Georgia stifled an eye roll as she headed up the trail. "Not like there are any interesting men."

Tanya's hiking boots crunched on the path behind her. "Clint Briscoe is back in the area."

At the thought of her handsome first crush, Georgia's chest tightened, but she said nothing.

"You heard me. Clint is back, and this time he's staying for good."

Georgia stepped over the exposed tree roots. "What do you mean, for good? I thought he lived in Nashville."

"His grandfather willed the land to him." Tanya caught up next to her and grinned. "The land that backs up to your family's property."

Georgia tamped down the excitement growing in her chest. She shouldn't get too enthusiastic. Clint probably wouldn't want anything to do with her. And even if he did, she didn't have a clue what she should do about it. "I thought his grandad was still alive."

"He is," Tanya said. "But between his heart attack and breaking a hip, he needed help. From what I hear, the deal is,

Clint takes care of him until he passes, then the property is his for good."

As they continued up the trail, two squirrels chattered and skittered through the underbrush.

"What about his brothers?" Georgia asked.

"You mean the Fireman and pro football star? Why would they want to live here?"

"Hey, those are fighting words." Georgia turned toward her friend and feigned a look of mock horror. "Garden Valley is the greatest city on Earth." At least as far as she was concerned. She'd ventured out into the big city when she attended college. For her, a tranquil and uncomplicated life in the Tennessee mountains was far more desirable.

"For us, anyway. Not so much for those who are looking for big city nightlife."

"Ugh." Georgia shuddered. "No, thank you." Quiet nights at home, reading a book or hanging out with friends, were her idea of having a good time. She continued walking, catching a glance of a distant peak through a break in the trees.

"Maybe you should welcome Clint to town."

"He probably doesn't even remember me. I haven't seen him since I was in high school."

Sunlight filtered through the dense canopy of trees, casting dappled patterns on the ground.

"You haven't seen one another in a few years," Tanya said, "but you've blossomed since then."

"Blossomed? I thought I was kind of decent-looking by then." At least she was no longer the gangly, gawky mutant like in middle school. Georgia sped up, wishing she could leave those awful memories behind.

"Don't get me wrong, you've always been gorgeous, but your womanly curves got curvier after graduation."

"Thank you. I think," Georgia said. "Since you're my best friend, you see the best in me. You know as well as I do, I was not attractive when I was younger." Her grandmother and mom were the beauty queens, not her.

"Take it as a compliment. And yes, you had your ugly duckling moments, but you turned into a swan."

Georgia tripped over a rock. "I don't think I'll ever hit swan level, but thank you. If it weren't for braces, my front teeth would still stick straight out from my face. And yes, I had little to show in the front section until after high school graduation. Thank you for those not-so-fond memories."

"God was trying to keep you out of trouble," Tanya said. "If you had been well-endowed in school, you would have had to beat the guys off with a stick. I mean, other than the time you smacked Magilla Macintosh."

"Ugh. That behemoth of a bully had it coming."

"Yes, he did. And thank you for standing up for me."

Georgia glanced over her shoulder. "It's the least I could do since he was trying to kiss you."

"You saved me from a fate worse than death. At the tender age of five, I did not want to have my first kiss tainted by a slobbering, silly boy."

"Good thing you saved that kiss for Blake."

Tanya's eyes glazed over, and she got that dreamy-eyed look she got whenever Blake's name was mentioned. "Only God knew I would marry the boy in the hospital crib next to mine on the day I was born."

"It is rather disgusting that you two have been together so long and still love one another."

"Other than the few months when we broke up and dated other people." Sadness tinged Tanya's words.

Regret hit Georgia like a sharp pain, and she longed to go

back and change what happened. For two years, the guilt of her actions had weighed heavily on her heart. Even though God had already forgiven her, why did the memory of needing Tanya's forgiveness still haunt her?

Avoiding looking at her friend, Georgia spotted a boulder where they could sit and enjoy the scenery.

Tanya sat next to her. "Your man is out there somewhere."

Through the gaps in the trees, the valley below lay spread before them, a panorama of various shades of green.

"He's somewhere, but not here." Georgia gave a dramatic sigh. "Maybe I'll be like Melba and live alone. She's done okay on her own."

"Please don't be like Melba." Tanya dug out her water bottle and took a swig. "She's a sweet lady, but way too feisty for someone her age."

"I'd love to have half her energy."

"Mr. Grady says Melba drinks some homemade concoction she makes."

"Moonshine?" Georgia shot a glance at her friend.

"No, nothing alcoholic. He said he once tried it and his hair burst into flames."

Georgia's jaw dropped. "Mr. Grady is bald."

"Yep," Tanya deadpanned. "And that's how he said it happened."

Under the watchful scrutiny of his Pops and two dogs, Clint worked to fix the damaged fence. Someone had cut the barbed wire, and from the tracks leading away, they had been riding a four-wheeler.

We'd better check the rest of the fencing." Pop's gaze swept the area. "With all the thefts in the area, we need to make sure nothing else is damaged or missing."

Clint finished making the repairs and put the tools in the back of the old pickup. "Have you heard anything about the thefts?" He gave a head scratch to the two dogs who were obviously enjoying being lazy, hanging out in the vehicle's bed.

"The rumor mill is running wild," Pops said. "Some think it's the people who are moving into the new neighborhoods around town. Others are blaming it on a group of mischievous teenagers. Grady says it's Bigfoot."

Clint stifled a chuckle as he slid back into the driver's seat and drove along the fencerow. "Well, the creature has been on its feet for generations. Maybe he's getting too old to get around on those enormous feet of his."

"That could be the case. It just wouldn't be the same seeing the hairy critter using a walker." Pops grinned. "Not that it wouldn't be disturbing picturing him driving through the forest on a four-wheeler or a motorcycle."

"Do the police have any ideas?"

"Not that I've heard. They and Georgia Shaffer are looking into the thefts."

At the name of the cute girl he'd enjoyed seeing over the summer, Clint shot a surprised look at Pops. "Georgia? Does she work with the police?"

"Kinda. She's a private eye."

"You're kidding? In Garden Valley?"

"She works at her dad's business. You remember Shaffer's Outfitters? They also do private investigations."

Clint shook his head. Surely there wouldn't be that big a need for a private eye in the little town. Sure, it had almost tripled in size since he was here last time. But picturing someone as attractive as Georgia doing that kind of work didn't seem logical. "So, she works for her dad. Is she married?"

Pop's attention jerked toward Clint, and his eyes got a mischievous sparkle. "She's still single and even prettier than the last time you were here. You need to give that girl a call."

Clint punched the accelerator. He wouldn't risk his heart again, no way, not after what happened the last time.

Despite it all, he smiled at the memory of the kisses he'd once shared with Georgia.

# *Chapter 3*

Monday morning, Georgia stepped inside one of her favorite places, Garden Valley's General Store. The historic two-story building housed an eclectic mix of groceries, hardware, and souvenirs, along with homemade items from local artisans and an old-fashioned soda fountain.

The bell on the general store door announced her arrival as she stepped inside. The old wooden floors creaked under Georgia's feet as she bypassed Tommy, the small boy known for his mischievous acts, drooling over the candy section of glass jars filled with colorful, nostalgic goodies.

At the soda fountain, Georgia sat on a round cushioned seat upholstered in durable red vinyl.

"Hey, Sweet Pea." Melba, with her silver hair pulled back in a ponytail, grinned. 'What can I get you?"

Georgia returned the grin to the older woman who refused to tell anyone her age. Rumor had it that Melba was older than the hills but still growing strong. "I'll have a root beer float."

"Wise choice, young one. Who needs coffee early in the morning?" Melba chuckled as she turned away and got to work.

In the mirror behind the soda fountain, Georgia watched other tourists and customers milling about the store. A couple about her age walked hand in hand. An older, smiling couple talked in quiet tones as they stood by the candy section.

"So, anything new in your world?" Melba asked.

"Not really."

Melba handed Georgia her root beer float. "Really?" Her

expression was pure mischief, embodied in her grin. "I heard someone new had moved to our area."

Georgia, understanding the context of the conversation, took a slow sip of her drink. "With all the new construction and the town's growth, new people are moving in every month."

"Oh, good grief," Melba said. "You know who I am talking about. Clint Briscoe. He's moved to his pop's farm. Have you seen him lately?"

At the thought of Clint, warmth crept onto Georgia's cheeks. "Not in years."

"He was cute then, but oh baby, he has become even more handsome," Melba fanned her face. "If I were younger, I'd be after that man. You need to go and see him. He needs to see what he's been missing."

Georgia huffed out a scoff. "Right. As though he'd be interested."

"You don't give yourself enough credit. You're a beautiful young woman."

Georgia wasn't sure what to do with compliments. In her mind, she still felt like the awkward kid she'd been throughout her early years.

In the mirror behind the soda fountain, Georgia cringed when she spotted Beatrice Finklebine entering the store. The Community chairwoman, a gossip and busybody, the only child of Colonel Finklebine, seemed to have only one goal in life: making as many people as possible as miserable as she was.

Beatrice walked straight toward Georgia. Her sensible-clad shoes tapped an impatient staccato beat on the wooden floor. "Have you or Tanya found Jake's four-wheeler yet? Or any of the other missing items?" She huffed.

Georgia tried to put on a pleasant expression as she faced the woman. "Not yet. We're still working on it."

"Give the girl a break, Beatrice," Melba said. "Investigations take time."

Beatrice's nose wrinkled in disgust. "This doesn't concern you, Melba Marshall."

Eyes narrowed to slits, Melba drew up to her full five-foot-four height. "Beatrice Finklebine, you are a ... a ... an evil woman!"

Beatrice gasped and put a hand on her ample hips. "Because I want thieves brought to justice?"

"No, because you're always putting your nose in business that isn't yours. You're probably the thief!"

"Slander!" Beatrice pointed her bony finger.

Melba ran from behind the counter, and Georgia grabbed her drink and considered running for cover. The two women's battles were legendary in Garden Valley.

"Homewrecker! Melba screamed.

"Floozy," Beatrice countered.

The barbs flew back and forth as the women stood face-to-face. If they had been cats, the fur would have been flying to the two-story ceiling.

"Ladies!" General Store owner and manager, Oswald Chambers. Stepped between the women. "Dagnabit." He stamped his foot. The silver-haired, plump man with a normally sweet expression huffed. "Stop this nonsense right now. I can hear you both hollering from my office. You two have got to get over your feud."

Melba muttered something under her breath. Beatrice did the same.

Oswald held up his hands. "Stop it! We have visitors here. Tourists and townspeople who are looking for a peaceful place to shop."

Both women straightened and plastered on pleasant

expressions as though nothing had happened. Melba went back behind her counter, and Beatrice disappeared down one of the store aisles.

"Sorry about that, folks," Oswald turned to the wide-eyed people standing nearby. "Just part of the show. Free sodas for everyone in the store."

As people crowded around the soda fountain, Georgia finished her drink, paid, and quietly left.

As a private eye, she'd take any case, except for getting entangled in the ongoing drama between those two women.

Trying not to curse, Clint stared at the empty space in the barn where he'd parked the four-wheeler. He didn't move it, and Pops sure didn't.

Clint glanced over his shoulder at the two dogs staring at him from the barn doorway. "What happened? Weren't you two on guard duty last night?"

Butch, the Great Pyrenees, sprinted off, while Dash, the Border Collie, approached Clint with a low-wagging tail.

Seriously? Guard dogs that don't guard.

Clint patted the collie. "I'm not mad at you. I'm mad at the thief."

A muffled woof came from outside the barn. Butch, a scrap of fabric dangling from his jaws, dashed toward Clint and dropped it at his feet.

Clint picked up the torn cloth of what looked like someone's jeans pocket. "Good job, Butch. Looks like you took a bite out of the criminal."

Butch stood up taller and let out a woof.

He gave the dog a good petting, then, with a sinking feeling,

Clint followed the tracks of the stolen four-wheeler to the place where the fence had been cut.

Frustrated, he let out a growl, took his phone out of his back pocket, and dialed the police.

# Chapter 4

Clint berated himself as he drove the two-lane winding road toward town. He should have locked the barn. The annoying fact was that no one in the area even considered locking their barns before these thefts.

Who was stealing vehicles and why? And why hadn't the police found who was responsible?

As he neared a sharp curve, he tapped his brakes to slow his speed. As a teenager, he'd hit the side of Pop's pickup against the guardrail when he took the curve too fast. Pops didn't mind and said it only added character to the old truck, but Clint's dad had been furious.

At the thought of his father, Clint tried to tamp down the rising anger. He'd never been good enough or fast enough for his strict coach dad. He never measured up to his dad's standards since his brothers were both taller and bigger than Clint's five-foot-eleven frame. He didn't even measure up to six feet.

Reining in his thoughts, Clint focused on the road in front of him. A scenic overlook revealed rolling ridges fading into the blue haze. At least here in the hills, valleys, and mountains of Tennessee, he felt at home.

The road leveled out and straightened as he neared Garden Valley. Clint drove around the square. He couldn't believe the transformation of the small town since his last visit. The refurbished buildings now housed bright, colorful storefronts for new businesses.

The downtown area was filled with people of all ages, some walking, others chatting in small groups. When did the town become a tourist destination? At least the general store looked the same. Maybe he'd stop by the soda fountain and get something to drink after he ran his errands.

Clint parked in front of the courthouse and stepped out of his truck. As his gaze swept the area, the sight of the blonde woman seated at a table outside the new cafe caused a sudden, sharp pain in his chest. She looked way too much like his old girlfriend.

He internally groaned at the memory of the relationship he thought would last forever. He'd bought a marquis-cut engagement ring and rented an event venue on a farm outside of Nashville to arrange the surprise for his girlfriend. Friends and family had been invited. He'd even hired a band, a photographer, a videographer, and contracted barbecue to feed the seventy-five people who hid in the wings waiting for him to pop the question.

Clint arranged for his best friend to bring his girlfriend to the event, ensuring she remained completely unaware of the surprise. When they arrived, Clint got on his knee, held out the ring, and proposed.

His girlfriend stood there for a moment, then, with a quick apology, left with Clint's best friend. They married two weeks later.

Clint rubbed the ache in his chest. Noticing what he'd refused to see, his mother had gently cautioned him during the time he dated his girlfriend. He'd ignored the signs, the warnings about his girlfriend and so-called best friend.

After the embarrassing failure, his dad and brothers were far from kind when discussing the incident. At least his mother prayed for Clint then and continued to pray for him.

For that, he was grateful. His mom's prayers seemed to reach where his couldn't.

Clint pulled his shoulders back. He wouldn't make that mistake again. He'd work on the farm, take care of Pops, and stay far away from women.

The low hum of conversation, ringing phones, and the clatter of keyboards drifted from beyond Tanya's police station cubicle.

Georgia sat in the hard chair across from her friend's desk. "What have you got?"

Tanya's professional look was pulling her shoulder-length, straight, light brown hair into a ponytail. "I have a lead. Last night, a flatbed truck hauling a four-wheeler was spotted on the interstate leading toward Virginia."

"Do you think that's a theft from our area?"

"Maybe," Tanya said, her face serious, but her eyes betrayed a hint of mischief. "We got a call this morning that a four-wheeler was stolen last night."

"That's sad about the theft, but great that someone spotted the truck. Did they get the license plate?"

"Only the first few numbers. We're searching on that lead, and the state patrol is keeping watch."

"Whose four-wheeler got stolen?"

"Ours." Clint Briscoe, with his brown eyes, light brown hair, and a soft hint of a nicely trimmed mustache and beard on his handsome jaw, stood in the cubicle's doorway.

Oh, my goodness, he looked better than ever. *Oh, baby.*

Clint's gaze moved toward Georgia. A spark of recognition seemed to flash in his eyes before he turned his attention back to Tanya. "They cut our fence and took it last night. Have you any leads?"

"I was just telling Georgia — you remember Georgia, right?" Tanya grinned as her gaze went back and forth between them.

Clint dipped his head in response. "Sure." His gaze flicked to Georgia, and a slight smile played on his lips. "I remember her."

Feeling a touch faint at his positive response, Georgia averted her eyes to stare at anything other than her handsome, long-lost friend. A vivid memory of kissing him sent a jolt of heat up Georgia's spine, flushing her face.

Tanya, still grinning from ear to ear, cleared her throat. "So anyway, we are on the case."

Clint placed a piece of torn denim cloth on the desk. "One of our dogs tried to stop the thief."

Tanya surveyed the material. "That might help narrow down our search." She gave a light chuckle. "We'll look for someone missing a back jean pocket who probably has a very sore rear."

He nodded. "I hope you find him soon. When I called, I was told I needed to fill out some form or something."

"Right," Tanya got to her feet. "Let me get those for you." She hurried away.

Georgia gazed up at Clint. "I heard you were moving to the area." Her hand moved absent-mindedly to cover her birthmark.

"Yeah, I'm taking over Pop's farm. Taking care of him, I mean, until..." Clint's voice became quiet, and a vulnerable look crossed his face, as if trying not to think of his grandfather passing.

The overhead lights buzzed and flickered as though concerned about his reaction.

"Your Pop is still young, right?" Georgia tried to give a reassuring smile.

"Yeah, he is," Clint nodded as relief crossed his face. "He's going to be okay for a long time."

"I think he's only a year older than my grandmother."

"That's right. How's she doing?"

"Okay. Grandmother still looks great, but I can tell she's sometimes lonely."

"Yeah, I see that in Pops, too." Clint's chocolate brown eyes met hers, and she sensed a deep, unspoken sadness within them.

From the next cubicle, a radio crackled with static, punctuated by muffled voices.

"I'm glad you're here," Georgia said. "Maybe we can get together sometime."

Clint swallowed hard and looked away. For a few seconds, she wondered if he wasn't as excited to see her as she was to see him. Finally, his eyes lifted to her. "That'd be nice."

Tanya walked back into the cubicle and handed Clint the paper and a pen. "Have a seat. You can fill the form out here."

He sat next to Georgia, and she breathed in the fresh, clean fragrance that always clung to Clint Briscoe. When he was younger, even after sweating, he still had an attractive, clean smell. Georgia tried not to lean closer while he filled out the form.

A big grin on her face, Tanya kept looking back and forth at them.

Georgia could tell her friend romanticized the moment, believing it was a destined reunion for the star-crossed lovers. Not that she and Clint had been lovers. Just a few kisses, which had never been enough. As more heat gathered on her cheeks, she fanned her face.

His gaze glanced toward her for a quick moment, and she

spotted the fun-loving teenager she'd once known.

Clint straightened and went back to filling out the form. Finished, he signed and handed the paper to Tanya. "Let me know if you need anything else." He got to his feet, and he looked at Georgia for a moment. "Good to see you."

Georgia smiled. "You too."

Clint took a step, stopped, and turned toward her. "Could I get your number?"

Georgia sprang to her feet, the sudden movement sending her chair crashing loudly to the floor. With a silent wish to sink into the earth, she hastily bent to pick up the chair.

His eyes sparkled with amusement as he helped to set the furniture upright. "Your number?"

"Right. Yes." For the life of her, she went blank. Totally blank and couldn't remember her name, much less her own phone number.

With a chuckle, Tanya handed a piece of paper to Clint with Georgia's number.

"Thanks." After glancing at both of them, he turned his smile toward Georgia. "I'll see you around."

Sweaty with mortification over the chair incident and her practically drooling over Clint, Georgia sank into the chair as he walked away.

"That went well," Tanya smiled. "Enough sparks were flying between you two to set off fireworks in the next county."

"Those weren't sparks. That was me combusting from embarrassment."

"Don't worry, you're cute when you turn beet red, glow with sweat, and fall over a chair."

Georgia put her head in her hands. Instead of being a klutz, why couldn't she be graceful and sophisticated? What would she do if Clint called?

Even worse, what if he never called?

# *Chapter 5*

Clint wiped his greasy hands on a stained rag. It had taken him an hour to get the old, smaller four-by-four running again. Thankfully, the ATV had been stored under a tarp in the barn where the thieves hadn't noticed.

He was still mad at himself for showing interest in Georgia. He didn't need a woman in his life. Hadn't he been through enough? He'd been humiliated, his heart run through a meat grinder, and left standing with people stunned into silence at his idiocy of thinking his girlfriend wanted to marry him.

Clint shoved a hand through his hair. And yet he wanted to see Georgia again. She'd been a cute teenager, but now she was gorgeous.

Man, he needed to stay busy, keep focused on helping Pops, and take care of the property.

"What did the police say?" Pops, leaning on his cane, stood in the barn doorway. The two dogs sat at his feet as though spectators.

"They're still working on it."

"So, what's troubling you?"

Clint pretended to look at the vehicle's motor again. "Nothing."

"You've got something on your mind. Just say it."

"I saw Georgia Shaffer." Clint glanced at his grandad.

A wide smile spread across Pops' face. "Ah, so that's what's got you all discombobulated. Georgia is a beautiful woman inside and out. Good family too. We're blessed to have our property back up to theirs."

Clint tried not to groan. Nothing worse than a woman temptation wrapped in a nice package located just over the next hill.

"You're overthinking things," Pop said. "That woman you dated, who I will not name, messed up your heart and your head, but that doesn't mean you should give up hope that God might have a better woman for you."

"It's not that easy," Clint kicked one of the vehicle's tires.

"Don't make life so hard. Pray and ask God for guidance."

"I did that before, and it didn't help," Clint growled.

"Did you pray before or after she who will not be named ran off?"

Clint used his rag to rub at a dark spot on the four-by-four. "No comment."

Pops hobbled next to him. "That other woman wasn't right for you. I know it hurt, probably still hurts." He laid a hand on Clint's shoulder. "But sometimes God pries things out of our hands because he has something better."

"Maybe," Clint mumbled. He wasn't ready to let go of the hurt and move on.

"Son, be open to the blessings God has for you."

Clint gave his Pops a quick nod. He might not be ready to dive into another relationship, but he didn't want to be miserable either.

Maybe he would give Georgia a call. It had been years since they spent time together. They'd been good friends when he visited in the summers.

Well, the worst outcome would be another round of humiliation, but this time with a different group of people watching.

Georgia stood behind the counter of Shaffer's Outfitters as a middle-aged guy with a cheesy grin flirted with her. To make matters worse, he was twice her age, twice her size, and he wore a wedding ring. She'd never understand why some men thought they could do as they pleased.

She glanced over her shoulder, hoping her dad would get back from the stockroom. Unfortunately, he still wasn't in sight.

The customer leaned closer, his enormous belly splayed over the counter, and made a lewd comment that made her recoil in disgust.

Georgia turned and calmly picked up the pepper spray she kept for such occasions. "Would you like a personal demonstration of how this works?"

The man gave a nervous chuckle as he took a step back. "No, not really."

Her dad, holding the black hiking boots the customer had requested, came from the back room and glanced between them. His eyes narrowed as he studied the man. "Sorry, we don't have boots in your size."

The customer gave him an incredulous look. "What are those in your hands?"

Her dad placed the boots on the floor, then, with his back ramrod straight, stepped closer to the man. "We don't cater to people like you."

"Like me?" The man huffed. "I'm a paying customer."

"Not in my store."

"I'll, I'll write a bad online review."

"You do that." Her dad's voice was deadly calm. "And I'll be happy to reply and share the lewd comment you made to my daughter."

The man's face flamed red, and he rushed out the door.

"I'm sorry you had to hear that," her dad said.

Georgia shrugged. "I've heard worse."

"What?" Her dad's face blanched. 'Who else has talked to you like that?"

"A few customers."

He let out a growl that made the hair on her arms stand at attention. "If anyone talks to you again like that, throw them out or tell me, and I'll throw them out."

She wasn't sure whether to laugh or salute. "Yes, sir."

"What is going on?" Beth, Georgia's mom, emerged from the back office, a smile on her face.

"Just a run-in with a slimy customer." Georgia shrugged.

"Oh, I've had to deal with so many of those types," Beth waved her hand like it was no big deal.

Georgia had no doubts since her mom, at forty-three, was still a beautiful woman.

"What!" Her dad looked horrified. "Why didn't you tell me?"

"Because you would beat them to a pulp."

He clenched his fists. "You bet I would!"

Beth laid her hand on his chest. "Honey, it's okay. If anyone gets out of hand, we will tell you," her gaze went to Georgia. "Right?"

"Right. Besides that, I've only had to use the taser on one man."

"I used a taser on two men and pepper-sprayed three," Beth stated casually.

Her dad stumbled back, steadying himself against the wall. "What happened to my sweet, innocent women?"

Georgia grinned. "Dad, you taught us to take care of ourselves."

Beth gave him a big kiss. "That's right, honey." A seductive glint mixed with a mischievous twinkle in her smile. "So, you better watch yourself."

Her dad gave her mom a big embrace. "I am one lucky man."

With hands intertwined, they moved to the back, their giggles erupting in waves.

Georgia sighed and leaned against the counter. Someday, maybe she'd have a marriage like her parents.

Until then, she'd keep the pepper spray and taser handy, and pray God would send her a good man. Preferably, one named Clint Briscoe.

# *Chapter 6*

Working in an office had made him a wimp. He needed to man up. Clint rubbed the sleep still in his eyes.

He'd gotten up before sunrise to make the rounds to check the fence and the pastures. Fortunately, the fencing was intact; the cows looked healthy, and the new calves were nursing without issues. The clean, full watering troughs reflected the sunlight, while the small creek on the property gurgled with crystal-clear water.

In the next week, he'd need to rotate the cows to the other pasture. A breeze rustled the trees above where he stood. He loved being outside, enjoying the buzz of insects, the croaks of frogs, and the lowing of cattle.

Since he was a kid, he'd dreamed of having a place like this. Pop's farm was the perfect blend of rolling pastures with a backdrop of the Smoky Mountains.

Even though Pops had sold much of his herd after his injury, the remaining grass-fed cattle should fetch a good amount at auction. Thankfully, Clint had a healthy savings account from his former employer to offset any additional farm expenses. But, boy, it was nice not to have to go into an office and sit behind a desk.

The smell of bacon wafted on the breeze. Clint quickened his pace, envisioning breakfast and coffee waiting at the farmhouse. He went through the back door and pulled off his worn boots.

Hearing the rumble of Pop's voice mixed with the softer

tones of a woman, Clint paused. Tiptoeing toward the sound, he peeked around the doorway leading to the kitchen.

At the stove, next to Pop, stood Georgia's grandmother, Janis Lucas. The woman was a year younger than his grandad and, at sixty-seven, still in great shape. Even in jeans and a casual top, she had a regal look about her.

Through their lighthearted conversation as they prepared breakfast, it was clear there was a mutual attraction.

Well, what do you know? His old Pops still had a swagger about him.

Unsure of what to say, Clint cleared his throat.

Pops and Janis whipped around, their startled glances implying they had been caught doing something they shouldn't have.

"Clint!" Pop said more loudly than necessary. "Come on in. Janis is fixing breakfast and brought some cinnamon rolls for us."

"Thanks, Mrs. Lucas." Clint stepped into the kitchen. "That's very kind of you."

"No need to be formal. You can call me Janis." Her blue eyes seemed to have a sparkle about them as her gaze went toward Pops. "The cinnamon rolls are the least I could do. Wayne mentioned you liked them."

Pop's posture was more erect than usual, and his chest puffed out slightly, as if he were trying to impress Janis.

"Breakfast is almost ready," Pop said. "Have a seat, and we'll bring it over."

Seated at the already set table, Clint watched as the couple spoke in hushed but sweet tones to one another.

Watching Pops with another woman was strange, but surprisingly didn't make Clint uncomfortable. Pops had loved his wife well until her passing. He deserved to be happy.

Then again, what if Pops married again? Where would they

choose to live, and what would happen to the farm? And would it be weird if Clint went out with Georgia?

Janis placed a plate filled with bacon, sunny-side-up eggs, toast, and a big, frosted cinnamon roll in front of Clint. "I hope you enjoy the meal."

He had to swallow to keep from drooling. "Thanks, this looks amazing."

Pops held out the chair for Janis, took the seat next to her, and said a nice prayer blessing the meal.

"Clint," Janis said as she placed a napkin on her lap. "It's good to have you back in town."

"It's good to be here. I've missed the farm and the surrounding area."

"We are blessed to live in such a beautiful place." She ate a bit, swallowed, and then gracefully dabbed her mouth with a napkin. "I hope you and Georgia can get together."

Judging by the playful glint in Janis' eyes, Clint knew exactly what she meant.

At the thought of Georgia, heat crawled up his back and settled on his neck. Hoping to cool off, Clint took a big swig of cold orange juice.

Why had his body reacted like that? He hadn't seen Georgia in years, yet he had never forgotten her. Their time together was unforgettable. Georgia wasn't only beautiful; she had a great personality, was loads of fun, and a fantastic kisser.

While Pops and Janis talked, Clint dug into his breakfast. Avoiding every woman wasn't necessary.

Showing interest in a nice woman like Georgia would be okay. They could just be good friends, with perhaps a few friendly kisses.

Tanya knocked on Georgia's open door and stepped inside her office. "We should have another ATV theft tonight."

Georgia motioned to her friend to have a seat. "How can you be sure?"

Tanya sat across from Georgia's desk. "The police department is placing one as bait."

Georgia couldn't recall any police vehicles like that being used. "I didn't know the department had an ATV."

"We don't. We're using my dad's as bait over on Melba's farm. We just left it outside her barn. This time we'll catch the thieves. "

"I don't understand. If it's stolen, how are you going to catch them?"

"We've installed hidden security night vision cameras around Melba's property and also placed a tracker on the ATV."

"What if the thieves don't come?"

"I'll be surprised if they don't. Melba is talking up a storm about the ATV that a friend gave her. Even showing pictures to people who come in to shop or visit the soda fountain."

Georgia chuckled, imagining the woman gushing to everyone who entered the store. "Melba does realize that's only a loan, right?"

Tanya's brows furrowed. "I think I made that clear." Her expression brightened. "Want to do the stakeout with us? My dad, Blake, your dad, and Chief Carter have all agreed to be there."

"Sounds fun. Do I get to carry my gun?"

Tanya smiled and shook her head. "No, you'd better leave that at home. But you can bring your taser and pepper spray."

"Woot! Even more fun. I'll dress in camo and bring my night-vision goggles."

"Great. Meet at the police station at ten tonight." Tanya stood. "The Chief will go over the plan, and we'll head over to Melba's place. I already know you'll be with me."

"Oh, boy. A stakeout with my bestie. Wait, why aren't you going to be with Blake?"

Tanya gave an eye roll. "Hubby wants to be with the Chief stationed closer to the ATV."

"He wants to get in on the action, huh?" Georgia could envision the big man as a striking and intimidating presence in the dark.

"Definitely. Blake's hoping to do something manly and impressive. He's already laid out his long-sleeve black shirt, black jeans, and even had black face paint ready."

"Wait, why is there a stakeout if you want to track the ATV? Wouldn't you want them to take it?"

"Yes, but we also want to get eyes on who we are dealing with. Find out how they are stealing and transporting the vehicles."

"So, no one is going to jump out and handcuff them?"

"Probably not. Provided nothing goes wrong."

After her friend left, Georgia leaned back in her chair. She couldn't wait to be on another stakeout.

This time, she would eat a filling dinner to avoid stomach growls. She'd lather on the bug spray so she wouldn't be itchy all night. And she'd make sure to use the restroom beforehand, preventing another embarrassing dash into the woods or requesting to use someone's facilities.

This time, she would be quiet as a mouse, have a full tummy, take bug precautions, have an empty bladder, and be more professional. At least she hoped that would be the case.

# *Chapter 7*

Standing under the trees near Melba's house, Georgia reviewed her mental checklist. She'd used plenty of bug spray, was wearing camouflage, drank sparingly all day, had a nutritious dinner, and her bladder was empty. She was ready to go.

The team members were in their positions. Georgia and Tanya's dad were stationed close to the main road. Tanya's husband, Blake, was paired with Chief Carter behind the shrubs near the ATV.

The air at night felt great, except for the strong, whipping wind. Maybe that would blow away any bugs. Georgia wrestled the black cover she'd brought for the stakeout onto the ground behind a tree.

Tanya helped her wrangle the flapping blanket into submission. "Looks like you're getting ready for a picnic," she whispered.

Georgia kept her voice quiet. "You know if I sit on the ground, every creepy crawly within a mile will attack me."

"True, but you don't smell too weird. Did you forget your bug spray?"

"No, I'm good." Georgia sat and tried to get comfortable. "I'm using a new concoction that's not as odiferous."

"Good thing." Tanya moved next to her. "I hope it works. I don't want you scratching all night like you did that other time."

"Besides the bugs, how could I have possibly known I was sitting in poison ivy?" The leaves and branches above Georgia shook in the wind, almost as if laughing at her.

Tanya gave a light chuckle, as did a few others on the team. Georgia tried not to groan. She should have remembered they were all linked and could hear one another's conversation.

Each team member had earpieces with radio receivers clipped to their belts or pockets. Although the Garden Valley Police Department was small, they had access to modern, high-tech equipment courtesy of SAU Tech.

To make a more tempting target for thieves, Melba had turned off the lights both inside and outside her house.

Georgia put on her night-vision goggles and scanned the area and the towering trees surrounding them. No telling what was on the ground or lurking above.

She knew all too well that possums, raccoons, and other varmints roamed the night. Hopefully, all the sleeping snakes had found a place to coil up far away from where she was seated.

Georgia scanned the ground and the surrounding trees again. She'd once had a snake drop from a limb in front of her while she was walking in the forest. Her body shivered at that unwelcome thought.

The rhythmic chirping of crickets faded as the deep hoot of an owl echoed through the night.

"Heads up," Tanya's dad's voice said. "Vehicle approaching."

"False alarm," Georgia's dad replied. "Vehicle kept going."

Georgia readjusted to keep her focus on the ATV. "If the thieves come tonight, I hope they don't wait too late."

"You have other plans?" Tanya grinned.

"No. It would just be nice to wrap this case up before dawn."

"I second that motion," Georgia's dad said. Affirmation grunts came from the rest of the team.

A blast of wind caused a flurry of leaves and twigs to fall

from the branches above. Something struck Georgia's head. She lifted her hand to her hair and felt a flutter of movement against her fingertips.

Jolting to her feet, Georgia stifled a scream. It was moving!

Tanya jumped up. "What is it?"

"Something's in my hair!" Georgia whisper screamed as she clawed at the tangle of curls. "Get it out! Get it out!"

Tanya tried to help, but her efforts were lost in the wind's howl and Georgia's rising panic.

Voices came across the comm link asking what was happening. The sound of thumping feet was followed by a blinding light.

"What's wrong?" Blake whispered, his flashlight beam pointed at her face.

Blinded and panicked, Georgia threw off her night-vision goggles. "I think a snake fell on me!"

The hands of her friends tugged, pulled, and raked through her hair, then stopped.

A deep chuckle came from Blake. "Is this your snake?"

Georgia braced herself, anticipating seeing a colossal, wriggling serpent. Instead, Blake held an exhausted-looking lizard, its tiny claws barely gripping his finger.

"Poor little thing," Tanya said. "I can't imagine the trauma he went through."

Georgia's mouth dropped open. "You feel sorry for the lizard? He's the one who attacked me."

"Surely not," Blake said. "I think he's the one who sells insurance." He carried the lizard to a tree nearby and let it go. "See you in the commercials, little buddy."

"With friends like you two, who needs enemies?" Georgia muttered.

"Back to your stations," the chief's chuckling voice said

over the comm link.

Georgia took a few calming breaths. Okay, so it wasn't a snake. But still, it was slithering, and it had attacked. Nature still was conspiring to get her. Why had she thought she could go on another stakeout?

A surge of unease washed over her as the urgent call of her bladder became impossible to ignore. She crossed her legs.

Tanya growled. "Really? Now? You need to go to the bathroom now?"

Georgia whimpered. "Too much excitement."

Groans came from the men in her earpiece.

"Go to Melba's house," her dad's voice said. "I'll send her a text that you're coming."

"Thanks, Dad." Georgia gave Tanya an apologetic look. "Sorry."

Georgia, moving as silently as a shadow, raced through the trees and to the back of the house. The door opened, and Melba motioned her inside.

"Land's sake, Georgia. You must have the tiniest bladder on the planet." Melba motioned toward the bathroom. "Hurry and get back out there."

"Yes, ma'am. I'm so sorry." Georgia wasted no time attending to her business. Finished, she apologized again and ran out of the house and back into the tree line.

"Heads up. Vehicle approaching," Tanya's dad's voice announced.

"Coming closer," Georgia's dad whispered.

The rumble of a vehicle grew louder, and Georgia dove behind a tree. How could she get back to her spot without being seen?

"Stay put," Tanya's voice urged.

With her heart thumping like a drum, Georgia was sure the

sound would alert the entire world.

Though the engine idled, the truck remained motionless, a standstill that felt like ages. A dog barked in the distance.

Total silence came from the comms. What was going on? A faint rustle nearby made her hair stand on end.

From her crouching position, Georgia peeked out from behind the tree. A man stood next to the ATV, getting it ready to move. She knew him! He was the slimy customer from the other day at the shop.

A nearby branch snapped. She turned.

A hand clamped over her mouth, silencing her scream.

## *Chapter 8*

Georgia's life flashed through her mind. The problem was that it was nothing but every mistake she'd made. Right then, she promised God that if He helped her escape, she would finally address what happened two years ago with Tanya.

Georgia whimpered as a deep, gravely, smoke-filled voice whispered in her ear. "You scream, I will hurt you."

The hand slipped from her mouth, followed by a sharp tug on her hair, hoisting her up from her kneeling posture, causing her to spin around.

In front of her stood a hairy, bearded man, reeking of alcohol and cigarette smoke.

Bigfoot did exist!

Georgia tried to be brave, tried to look tough, wanted to fight back, use her taser or pepper spray, but her body stood paralyzed.

A wicked grin spread across the man's hairy face as his dark eyes raked over her. "Looks like we might have more than just an ATV to take back on this job."

"Not on my watch, you don't." The ominous sound of Blake's voice came from the darkness.

With a swift movement, the man whirled around, his gaze darting about.

Blake's fist connected with the man's jaw in a single, brutal blow, sending the man crumpling to the ground.

Georgia's legs turned to jelly, and she frantically reached out to the nearest tree for support. It was over. She was safe.

"I got you." Blake's arm steadied her. "Team, I have Georgia. She's safe."

"We have the other man," Chief's voice said over the comm.

Tanya's joyful cry echoed as she ran up and wrapped her arms around Georgia. "I'm so grateful you're okay."

Georgia buried her face against her friend's shoulder, tears falling hot and salty as relief surged through her.

"Next stakeout," Tanya whispered in Georgia's ear. "I'm making you wear those pull-up pants, the kind toddlers use, so you can stay put and not have to go to the bathroom."

Georgia wiped her tears. "After what just happened, I might just do that."

Blake seized the man, yanking him upright with a grunt. Tanya handcuffed him, and the man stumbled as they pushed him away.

Georgia's dad came running, his arms open wide for a bear hug that almost squeezed the breath right out of her. "I was praying like crazy."

She stayed in her dad's strong arms until, desperate for breath, she squirmed out of her dad's overzealous embrace. "I'm okay." Though a little wobbly, she tried to look tough. "He didn't hurt me."

"Promise me you won't go on another stakeout." The sight of her dad's teary-eyed look caused her throat to constrict. Her dad hardly ever showed emotion.

Georgia bit her lip. "I won't make that promise, but I will be more careful next time."

His eyes watery, he groaned as he studied her. "You're my little girl. I'd die if anything happened to you." He blew out a breath, then wrapped an arm around her shoulders. "Come on, let's get you home."

The next morning, Georgia put her head in her hands as she sat in her office desk chair. She'd barely slept between the adrenaline of what happened and what might have happened.

In the two hours she'd been in the office, her mom and dad had been in and out, checking on her every few minutes. Even Tanya had called to share the latest news and to ensure Georgia was doing all right.

She shuddered, trying to shake off the memory of the man's hairy, evil face. Why couldn't she move? Why had she stood there frozen in place? Why didn't she at least put up a struggle? What if Blake hadn't rescued her in time? What if that man *had* kidnapped her? What if ...?

Georgia's head swam with the worst-case scenarios, a dizzying whirlwind of potential negative outcomes.

She blew out her breath. Thankfully, God had rescued her, but now she needed to keep her promise and address what she'd done two years ago. Her stomach knotted at the thought.

She'd pleaded with God for forgiveness. Wasn't that enough? In some ways, yes. She knew God had forgiven her, yet a lingering ache in her heart hinted at a task God still desired of her—an apology to the person she'd wronged. The Bible was clear that forgiveness was essential for healthy relationships and spiritual well-being.

Shoving to her feet, Georgia stood. She needed to get moving and do something to outrun her thoughts and God's gentle nudge. Better yet, a root beer float from the soda fountain might help float away her worries.

Clint went into the general store, and the tiny bell above

the door chimed a welcome. He paused to check the list Pops had provided. From the ingredients, Clint hoped Janis would cook them another tasty meal. She'd been at the house yesterday afternoon, preparing Pop's favorite Italian dish.

Before Clint's grandmother passed away, she made Pops promise to marry again. At the time, Clint was surprised by the request, considering Pops' age. However, it made sense to see Janis with his grandfather. They made an attractive couple, and it was clear they cared for each other.

Steering the tiny shopping cart with a squeaky wheel ahead of him, Clint tried to focus on what he needed to buy. Pops had a good woman for decades, and the possibility of another.

Clint internally groaned. He couldn't even get one woman to love him. He thought his girlfriend would be the lasting love of his life, but that relationship ended in utter failure.

Rounding the aisle, he saw a group of people clustered around the soda fountain.

"I tell you, one man looked just like Bigfoot." Melba, the silver-haired woman, stood behind the counter, her hands moving as she spoke. "He was the hairiest thing I've ever seen. And I've seen some things."

A low murmur rippled through the crowd as they nodded in understanding.

"He tried to kidnap Georgia." Melba punctuated that statement with a dramatic finger point. "That hairy varmint had evil intentions for our girl."

The crowd gasped.

*Georgia?* Clint jerked his cart around, the wheels squealing in protest, and hurried toward the group.

"If Blake hadn't come to her rescue," Melba continued. "No telling what would have happened to her."

The thought made Clint's chest tighten with suffocating

pressure.

"Then, come to find out, the ringleader works at SAU Tech as a cleaner," Melba said. "At night, he would go through the offices and cubicles, looking for photos of people who owned ATVs or other easily stolen vehicles. He and his buddy transported them across the state line to sell them in Virginia."

Clint glanced at his list and the few items in his cart. Forget the groceries. He had to make sure Georgia was okay. He should have called and made time to be with her—no more waiting.

His heart pounding with urgency, he parked the cart out of the way and bolted toward the door.

# *Chapter 9*

Georgia shook her head. Her parents were still worried about her and barely let her out of the building.

Reaching the general store, she turned and could see her mother and father standing at Shaffer's window, watching her.

Good grief. She was a grown woman.

Georgia jerked the door open and ran directly into a solid, very nice-smelling chest.

"Georgia!" Strong arms encircled her, holding her close. "Are you okay?" Her handsome friend's gaze, filled with concern, softened as it swept over her face.

Well, she was now. She nodded and happily nestled against him as her worries disappeared in his embrace.

"I heard what happened." Clint's palm slid up her back, drawing her closer. He kissed the top of her head. "Man, I wish I had been there to keep you safe."

She must be in a dream. Georgia sighed. Clint's fresh, clean scent, as if he'd just showered, wrapped around her. She did love a nice-smelling man. It had been years since she'd been in his arms. Years since they kissed, and oh, how she'd missed his kisses.

"Georgia Shaffer!" Melba's voice yelled. "Come over here."

Clint's groan matched hers as they pulled apart.

His chocolate brown eyes gazed into hers. "Can I see you later?"

Georgia smiled. "I would very much like that."

Clint's smile matched hers as he walked backward. "I've got

to pick up a few groceries." He bumped into the shelves and gave her an embarrassed grin. "I'll buy you a soda when I finish." He grabbed an already-filled cart and hurried down the aisle.

"Georgia Shaffer," Melba yelled. "Stop your gawking at the handsome man and get your skinny tail over here and tell these people what happened last night."

Heat rocketed to her face as Georgia realized the crowd had been watching.

*Talk about last night?* Her vision tunneled. She couldn't move, paralyzed by the haunting sights, sounds, and emotions she experienced in the evil man's grasp.

"Georgia?" Clint ran toward her and gently wrapped his arm around her shoulder. "It's okay. I've got you. Why don't we go for a walk?"

"Melba," He turned his head toward the woman. "I think those questions should be answered by someone else."

"Sure, honey." Her voice softened. "I understand."

Clint moved his grocery cart off to the side, then gently guided Georgia out of the store, across the street to the gazebo park area next to the county courthouse, and directed her to a bench.

On autopilot, she sat next to him, their shoulders touching. What was wrong with her? She wasn't a weak, wimpy woman. Why was last night still affecting her like this?

A cardinal landed in the grass and, with a twitch of its head, hopped closer as though curious, then flew away.

"You don't have to say anything if you don't want to," Clint's kind voice said. "But I'm here if you do want to talk."

Georgia let out a frustrated sigh. "I'm okay. I don't know why my body keeps reacting like this."

"When dealing with trauma, our bodies and brains need time to catch up," Clint whispered.

In Georgia's peripheral vision, she could see him watching her. She didn't want to be a damsel in distress. She wanted to be a strong, independent woman—a private eye who could handle any case. Then again, she'd never been in a situation like last night.

A shudder ran through her.

Clint put his arm around her shoulder. He didn't say anything, just let her rest and compose herself in his firm yet gentle embrace.

Being with him, she felt safe. Cherished. Oh, how she wished they shared a connection, a relationship including kissing and permanence.

A car horn beeped as it passed by on the road.

Georgia straightened and pasted on a smile. "Clint, thank you for your kindness."

"Of course. That's what friends are for."

Her smile grew wobbly, and her stupid lip even trembled. She didn't want just to be Clint's friend.

She'd been the ugly duckling throughout most of her younger life and still felt that way. What would someone as sweet and handsome as Clint want with her?

"Hey," Clint's gentle gaze held hers, and his arm tightened around her shoulder. "It's okay. We can sit here as long as you need."

Afraid she might cry, she nodded and looked away.

"I'm really sorry about what happened last night."

Still not trusting her voice, she gave a quick nod and swiped a stupid tear that escaped from the corner of her eye.

Clint's chest tightened at the sight of Georgia's tears. He

cleared his throat, trying to keep himself from being emotional, especially with the beautiful woman he was hoping to be with. She needed comfort and strength.

What had happened last night? Had Georgia been threatened, touched in an evil way? Volcanic heat surged up his back at the thought. Man, he'd like to smash the face of anyone who hurt Georgia.

She whimpered.

Clint loosened his tight grip on her shoulder. "Sorry. Did I hurt you?"

She shook her head. "No, it's okay." Her gaze swung toward him. "Oh, Clint, I'm so sorry. You left your cart. Don't you need to go back and get it?"

"Don't worry. You're more important." Why hadn't he stayed in touch with her? They had a special friendship during the summers when he visited Garden Valley. She was gorgeous inside and out.

Her eyes flicked toward his. "I'd better let you get back to your shopping." Georgia rose to her feet.

He stood beside her, wanting to reach out and pull her close again. "Would you still like to get something to drink?"

Her smile didn't quite meet her brown eyes. "I'd like that, but maybe later, okay?"

"Yeah, sure. I'll call you?"

"Okay."

As Georgia left him standing there, he felt like a piece of his heart had torn away and fallen to the ground.

## *Chapter 10*

Clint raised the ax again and split another log. Seeing Georgia upset twisted his insides. He wanted to know what happened to her last night, and he didn't.

Man, he had to stay busy, or he'd go crazy. The thought of that thief touching her made his blood boil.

"Just how much wood do you think we need?" Pops stood leaning against the side of the barn.

The two dogs sat beside him, their ears perked as though curious about Clint's answer.

Not sure how long Pops had been watching, Clint wiped the sweat off his forehead and shrugged. "Never know how cold this winter might be." He whacked another log, feeling the satisfying thud of the ax meeting wood.

"Well, at the rate you're going, you'll have enough chopped for us and the neighbors us. Want to tell me what's going on?"

Clint took a deep breath, blew it out. Tried to calm down. He wasn't in the mood to talk.

A distant, echoing caw of a crow broke the silence.

He glanced at Pops. "You heard what happened last night?"

"You mean the thieves getting caught? Our ATV was still intact, so it should be delivered in a few days after the police process everything."

"That's good. But you heard about Georgia? About that guy who almost kidnapped her?" Clint swallowed the bitter bile burning its way up his throat.

Pops grimaced. "Janis told me. They're all pretty upset."

"I saw Georgia when I went to the store. She's not handling it very well."

"Can't imagine that was easy for the girl."

"No." Clint set up another log and swung the axe with a grunt. The wood exploded in two, sending fragments flying through the air.

The dogs took off in chase, bringing back the pieces. Their tails wagged like furry flags of victory as they dropped them at Clint's feet. He gave each of them a thankful pat on the back.

"Janis thought," Pops said, "maybe you should give Georgia a call, see if she'd like dinner."

Clint nodded. "Yeah, okay, I'll finish up and call her." He was planning to do that anyway once he calmed down and showered.

Pops attempted to look innocent, but the mischievous glint in his eyes gave him away. "Janis dropped off a picnic basket with items Georgia likes, if you want to take that with you."

Clint grinned and shook his head. "You working on matchmaking?"

"I wouldn't think you'd mind with Georgia."

"No, I wouldn't mind at all." Not one bit.

Georgia sat at her office desk, the quiet hum of the computer the only sound as she tried to concentrate on the latest background check for SAU Tech. Unfortunately, her mind kept replaying what had happened last night, as well as her embarrassing, wimpy interaction with Clint.

As much as she enjoyed his attention, she didn't want to be seen as a weak woman. Mainly because she never saw herself that way. She'd been on other stakeouts with Tanya and had even interviewed people during investigations.

Georgia sat straighter. She'd even handled herself without a problem in fending off unwanted advances from flirty men in the store.

But was that because she knew her Dad was nearby? Her shoulders slumped. Was she tough only when someone was there to protect her?

On top of all her self-doubt, the nagging sensation persisted that she needed to apologize for her actions from two years ago.

Why couldn't it just go away? She'd tried to ignore what she'd done. Why did she make that promise to God about finally addressing it?

Georgia raked her hand through her thick hair. If she made that apology, admitted what happened, her best friend in the world might never want to see her again.

Argh! Why couldn't she get her brain to focus on the work she needed to be doing?

With a frustrated huff, Georgia closed the file, shut down her computer, grabbed her purse, and shoved out of her chair. She'd finish tomorrow. Maybe by then she'd have a semi-functioning brain.

Georgia followed the murmur of voices coming from downstairs. Leaning against the doorframe, she watched her parents and grandmother huddled together, as if they were in some clandestine meeting.

"We were going to ask her over for dinner," Georgia's mom said in a quiet voice.

Her grandmother's eyes went wide, and she shook her head. "You can't do that."

"Why not? Were you going to have her over?"

"No." Her grandmother looked away.

Dad huffed out a frustrated breath. "Well, then, why can't

we ask Georgia over?"

"You just can't." Grandmother leaned closer and whispered something Georgia couldn't make out from where she was standing.

After exchanging their whispered words, the broad smiles plastered on their faces showed that a mischievous plot was brewing.

Curiosity getting the best of her, Georgia stepped toward them. "What's going on?"

Nervous chuckles came from the group. Her father rushed to the fishing rod display and examined the rods as if they were brand new. Her mother hurried to the checkout counter and searched through the receipts, while Grandmother remained motionless, as if staying still would make Georgia unable to see her.

"So," Georgia narrowed her eyes as she stepped closer, "who's going to invite me for dinner?"

"Got to go." Grandmother waved as she ran out the door.

"Not tonight, honey," her mom said. "Something's come up. I'm sure you're tired and ready to get home."

What were they up to? Well, she could play this game. "I was planning on running an errand."

"No!" Her dad stumbled toward her, nearly tripping over his own feet. "I mean. Maybe run your errands on another evening. Or maybe we could do it for you?"

"Good idea." Mom's head nodded and kept nodding. "We'll be glad to run your errand for you. You probably need to get home."

Georgia crossed her arms. "I don't know what is up, but fine, I'll go home. All by myself. All alone." Head down, she shuffled toward the door. "Probably have an old sandwich on moldy bread." She sniffled, glanced over her shoulder. "All by myself."

As she drove to her cabin, Georgia puzzled over what was happening with her family. From their mischievous grins, it was obvious they weren't worried about her anymore.

Well, whatever it was, she didn't appreciate being left out of the loop. Besides that, she really had planned on running that errand. The weight of her needed apology clung to her shoulders like a blanket of wet cement.

Georgia entered her driveway, and her heart skipped a happy beat. Clint sat on the front porch rocker.

So, that explained the secret activities of her family. She would definitely thank them later for the very handsome distraction. Her errand-running apology could wait for another day.

Georgia parked her pickup and sighed, wishing she had taken a moment to look presentable before coming home. After what happened earlier, it was a good sign that Clint was here. At least he didn't run and hide in the hills after her damsel-in-distress moment.

Even though her heart was dancing a happy dance, she tried to act casual as she walked toward him. Goodness, he looked incredibly handsome in jeans and a light tan Henley shirt.

He stood, his gaze searching hers as she walked up the front steps. "Hope you don't mind. I thought you could use some company and dinner."

"That's sweet of you. Thank you." She stopped beside him. "Interesting that you have my grandmother's picnic basket."

Clint gave a soft chuckle. "Long story. But the food looks great."

Georgia unlocked her door and motioned him inside. "If my grandmother made it, I know it will be good."

"I agree." Clint picked up the picnic basket and stepped into her den. "Janis makes the best cinnamon rolls."

Georgia swung her gaze back to him. "And how exactly would you know that?"

The color drained from Clint's face. "I, uh, I mean, uh, she brought them for Pops."

"She did, did she?" Georgia raised an eyebrow. So, that explained why her grandmother had been so chipper the last few days. Pops and Janis. Who would have thought? They would make a cute couple.

"Great place you've got here." Clint's gaze scanned the interior of her cabin.

"Thanks." Georgia made a desperate, quick glance around the room. Thank goodness, she had cleaned her house before she went to bed last night.

Clint placed the basket on her dining table. "I was wondering if, after we eat, you might want to go with me on a short hike?"

She couldn't resist teasing him. "You're staying for dinner?"

Clint's brows furrowed. "I, uh, thought."

He looked so miserable, Georgia placed her hand on his arm. "I'm sorry. I was just kidding. I would love for you to stay, and if it isn't too dark when we finish, a hike sounds nice."

Clint's smiling gaze went from her face to where her hand remained.

She jerked her fingers off his arm and hurried to the kitchen cabinets to get plates.

"Can I help?" He came up beside her.

His clean scent and closeness caused Georgia's brain to shut down, and she could only fumble in silence with the dishes.

"Could I get the silverware?" Clint's tone had a hint of amusement.

Georgia opened the drawer in front of him and pointed to where she kept the knives and forks.

Clint's shoulder brushed against Georgia's while he collected the silverware, and she resisted the urge to move closer.

How easy it would be to snuggle up against the man she'd dreamed about since she was a teenager. At the thought of snuggling with Clint, sunburn heat ignited her cheeks.

Good grief, she needed to compose herself. Spending an evening with Clint Briscoe was a dream come true, but what would he think of her if she couldn't even formulate a cohesive sentence?

"Do you also need me to carry the plates?" He stood next to her, his gaze sparkling with humor.

How long had she been standing there daydreaming? Georgia swallowed an embarrassed whimper, grabbed the plates, and hurried to the table.

# *Chapter 11*

Georgia set the plates on the table, then unpacked the goodies from the picnic basket. Being the spoiled granddaughter of Janis Lucas was a blessing.

The basket being given to Clint to deliver meant Grandmother was trying to play matchmaker, which Georgia was more than happy with her grandmother's plan.

Her grandmother had sent her famous chicken salad wrapped in a cold pack, along with Georgia's favorite salt-and-vinegar potato chips and key lime pie for dessert.

"I hope you're okay with chicken salad." Georgia sat at the table across from Clint and handed him the container.

"I'm good with pretty much anything termed food. Unless it's liver."

"Then, you're safe with my family. There's not a liver lover in the bunch." With a full plate, she picked up her fork and then hesitated, unsure whether to say grace and bless the meal.

Clint's brown-eyed gaze met hers, and he shifted in his seat as though uncomfortable. "Um, do you want me to say a prayer?"

"Do you mind?" Georgia held her hand toward his.

He wrapped his fingers around hers and said a simple prayer blessing the food. With a quick squeeze, he released her hand and picked up his fork and dug into his food.

Unsure how to start the conversation, Georgia ate quietly, the food offering a brief distraction as she sought a topic to discuss. "So what did you do after college?"

"Worked in Nashville for an insurance group," Clint said.

Georgia waited for more information, but when it didn't come, she plowed onward. "Did you enjoy your job?"

He shrugged. "It was okay. Paid the bills."

"I bet living in Nashville was nice. Seems like there's always something going on there."

"It's a busy place. Too busy for me. I prefer the quiet." Clint took a bite and swallowed. His chocolate-brown gaze remained on her. "I'm not surprised you stayed here and became a private eye. When I visited in the summers, you were always busy looking for missing items or lost animals."

"I've moved past pet investigations. Then again, a few months ago, I tracked down Melba's missing hog. Porky pig."

"She named her pig Porky?"

"Of course she did." Georgia put on a serious expression. "Porky is the son of Hogzilla."

He chuckled. "You're kidding."

She pointed her fork at him. "We do not joke about our porcine population, Mr. Brisco."

A deep furrow creased Clint's forehead. "Okay. Good to know."

At his troubled expression, Georgia couldn't contain her grin. "I'm sorry. I was just kidding about taking pigs seriously. However, I did not joke about the names or about finding Porky."

Clint leaned toward her, his expression unreadable. "I used to win hide and seek at Pop's farm until one of the animals told my brothers where I was. I think it was the pig who squealed."

"Ha! Very funny, Mr. Briscoe."

Clint grinned. "Yes, Miss Shaffer, I can poke fun with the best of them."

Georgia munched on a potato chip as she surveyed her handsome, punny friend. They'd had fun when they were younger, and it was great to know he still had his sense of humor.

The sounds of the woods drifted in through the open window—crickets, a distant owl, the gentle rustle of leaves.

"I'm sorry I didn't come back in the summers after high school." Clint's eyes held apology.

"I missed you." She picked up a potato chip and avoided looking at him. He'd never know how much she'd missed him.

"I'm sorry I didn't come back sooner. Once we moved to Texas for Dad's coaching job, I stayed there for college. I thought about you and missed you, too."

Georgia swallowed the lump rising in her throat. Then, her stupid lip started trembling because Clint was so nice and handsome and the man of her dreams, and he had actually missed her. To hide her lip tremors, she pretended to take a drink of water.

"Your grandmother makes a great chicken salad," Clint said.

Still a touch discombobulated finding out that Clint had missed her, it took Georgia a moment to compose herself. "She'll be happy to hear that. She's been rather cheerful lately. I think she enjoys having a reason to cook for someone new."

"Pops has been much happier, too." Clint leaned back, his fork idly tracing circles on his plate. He glanced up at Georgia, his expression softening. "Are you... really okay? After what happened?"

At the thought of that hairy, evil man threatening her, Georgia hesitated, her fingers tightening around her fork. "I'm getting there. I keep thinking I should have done something different. Been braver. But I just froze."

"It's okay to be shaken up by what you went through." Clint's voice was gentle.

"Thank you." Georgia looked at him, searching his face for any sign of pity, but found only understanding. "I guess I always thought of myself as strong, not someone who needed rescuing."

He gave a small, reassuring smile. "We all need help sometimes. I'm just learning that myself. Being afraid doesn't mean you aren't brave and strong. Despite what happened, you keep going."

A quiet moment passed, but Georgia didn't feel uncomfortable. She felt seen and understood.

"Thank you for dinner," Clint said.

Georgia sent him a grin. "You're the one who brought it over."

"You didn't have to let me stay." Clint's smiling gaze moved from her eyes to her lips.

At the thought of them kissing, heat settled on Georgia's cheeks.

Clint cleared his throat and rose to his feet. "Still up for that walk?"

Trying not to fan her face, Georgia hurried to clear the table. "Yeah. I think some fresh air would do me good."

After they did a quick clean of the kitchen, Georgia grabbed a light jacket and met Clint at the door. Even in summer, the evening air in the mountains could have a touch of coolness.

Should she put on bug spray or take her chances? Sometimes the bugs didn't bother her as long as she didn't get too close to the woods. Hopefully, she'd be okay.

As they stepped outside, she took a deep breath, enjoying the scent of pine and the faint sweetness of wildflowers.

"You know, I used to dream about living somewhere like this," Clint said as he walked next to her. "Quiet, peaceful. A place where you can actually hear yourself think."

"It's home. I can't imagine living anywhere else."

Fireflies blinked in the late evening as they followed a narrow path that wound through the woods behind her cabin.

Clint glanced at her, his expression thoughtful. "You're brave, Georgia. Even when we were younger, I always thought you were fearless."

"Me? Why?"

"There wasn't a case in town you didn't jump in to solve. There were no missing pets on your watch. And when we hiked together, you always chose the hardest trail, and you climbed higher in that old tree than I ever did."

Georgia shook her head. "I'm not sure that qualifies me as being brave."

They reached a small clearing. Moonlight reflected off the leaves as it spilled through the trees. The wind whipped her hair around her face. Although she didn't love how it made her look, at least it kept the insects at bay.

Clint nudged her with his elbow, a spark of playfulness in his eyes. "You know, I could show you some self-defense moves."

Georgia puffed out a laugh. "You mean, in case another lizard attacks me on a stakeout?"

His mouth dropped open. "A lizard got you, too? And you've kept going?" He put a hand on his chest. 'Oh, man, you are so brave."

She playfully smacked his arm. "Alright, wise guy. Show me your best moves."

Clint stepped back, adopting a mock-serious stance. "Okay, lesson one." His hand clasped her wrist. "If someone grabs you like this."

"I scream."

He blinked a few times as though trying to get his bearings. "I guess you could do that too."

"Now? I could scream really loud." Georgia hid her grin. "A real ear-busting scream. Want me to do that?"

"Uh, no, not now. So, let me show you." His grip tightened just a touch on her wrist. "If someone grabs you like this, don't pull straight back. Instead, twist your wrist toward the attacker's thumb. That's the weakest part of their grip."

Georgia followed his instructions. She rotated her wrist, turning it so her thumb pointed up and then out, away from Clint's fingers. With a quick, smooth motion, she slipped her hand free.

"See?" Clint smiled. "By twisting toward the thumb, you break their hold. It's simple, but effective."

"That worked," she grinned, "but what if someone grabs me from behind?"

A tiny smile played at the corners of his mouth. "Okay. Let's see about that." He stepped behind her and, in a comforting embrace, encircled her with his arms.

Georgia stood still, feeling his closeness and inhaling the subtle, familiar scent of his clean smell.

"Ready to practice the next move?"

She shook her head. "What if I don't want to be rescued right now?"

A deep chuckle rumbled from his chest. "I think we could stand here for a little while."

Georgia leaned back against him. "Yes, I think we could."

The soft hum of crickets and the summer breeze, carrying the smell of warm earth, swirled around them as they stood together, enveloping her senses.

"I have another move that might help," Clint whispered against her ear.

"You do?" Georgia's voice squeaked at the soft timber of his voice.

He gently turned her to face him. "Perhaps some mouth-to-mouth would help resuscitate your brave lips."

Georgia grinned. "I think my lips need all the bravery they can get."

# Chapter 12

**W**alking on air. She was walking on air. With the door closed, Georgia shimmied and danced around her office.

Last night with Clint had been fantastic. They'd talked and kissed, and kissed some more. Then they walked a little more, kissed some more. And she didn't even get a single bug bite. Oh, my goodness, she was walking on air.

A tap on her door made Georgia freeze for a moment, then she hurried to sit in the chair behind her desk. "Come in."

Her grandmother stopped inside the office and sashayed toward Georgia. "Just wondered how you liked the food."

From her sly smile, Georgia knew that wasn't all her grandmother was wondering about.

"It was great. Thank you so much for sending chicken salad, since you know it's my favorite. And I really liked the delivery man you chose."

Grandmother smiled as she settled in the chair across from the desk. "I thought maybe Clint needed a little gentle prodding."

"You can prod him anytime in my direction." Georgia grinned.

"Wayne's been worried about Clint for a while. Wayne said, and I quote, the boy had his heart busted by a no-good woman."

Georgia mentally groaned at the thought of someone hurting Clint. It wasn't surprising he'd dated other women since he was so sweet and handsome. But thinking about him with other females stirred up a deep, twisting jealousy, which was odd since she'd never felt that way before.

Grandmother chuckled. "You should never play poker."

Georgia tried to refocus. "Poker? Why would you say that?"

"It was clear you were having some not-too-nice thoughts about the woman who hurt Clint."

"That obvious, huh?"

Grandmother smiled. "Oh, yes. It's probably a good thing she doesn't live in our area."

"Well, that is good news. Clint deserves someone who will treat him right."

"That's why we want you two to get together. You need a good man, and he needs a good woman."

Clint was a good man, but was she good enough for him? What if she were only a rebound after the love of his life left him? As her insecurities surfaced, Georgia's hand instinctively went to her birthmark.

"You're overthinking again," Grandmother said.

"Probably." Georgia sighed and forced her hand back onto the desk. "But what if Clint wants someone beautiful, smarter, funnier, different from me?"

"Oh, honey, I wish you could see yourself for who you truly are. Use that intelligent, investigative mind of yours to discover the truth."

Investigations she could handle, but investigating herself? How was that even possible? She didn't have a clue. "I still think I'm that klutzy mutant like I was in middle school."

"Well, you aren't that now. You are a beautiful, intelligent woman with a great sense of humor. Clint couldn't find anyone better."

Georgia pushed a stray hair behind her ear. "You're my grandmother. You're supposed to think stuff like that."

"Instead of thinking negatively, think positively. Clint likes you."

"I hope so, because I really, really like him. I've had a crush on him since we first met."

Grandmother chuckled. "I know that's true. Clint's back in town to stay, and he's interested in you. Enjoy your time together. We're praying for you and Clint."

Georgia quirked an eyebrow. "We?"

"Wayne and your parents are also praying."

"Got the whole town praying, do you?"

Grandmother grinned as she stood. "A good portion."

"Speaking of men." Georgia rose to her feet and stepped closer. "Are you getting serious about Wayne Briscoe?"

"Would that bother you?" Her grandmother looked genuinely concerned. "If I did?"

"Not at all. You were a great wife to Grumps. If you have another chance at love, go for it."

Grandmother's eyes glistened with tears, and her bottom lip quivered. "Thank you."

Georgia enveloped her sweet grandmother in a hug. "You're the best, and I want the best for you."

"As I do for you, sweet one."

"Hey, what's going on in here?" Smiling, Georgia's dad stood leaning against the doorframe. "Hugging on company time is never frowned upon. However, I have a request for Georgia." He turned his gaze toward her. "We're almost out of coffee and tea. Would you mind picking up some for the break room?"

Georgia grinned. "I'll be more than happy to run that errand." She gave her grandmother another quick hug, grabbed her purse, then fist-bumped her dad. "I'll be back soon." She definitely enjoyed running errands when she could get a root beer float.

A few minutes later, she stepped into the General Store.

Georgia stopped in her tracks. Raised voices near the soda fountain drowned out the usual clatter of cans and chatter.

Melba and Beatrice Finklebine were going at it again, their voices rising as accusations flew.

Hands on her hips, Beatrice stood in front of Melba. "Don't you dare call me a liar! I know what you did with Harold behind the bandstand during the Peach Festival of '72."

Melba's face flamed red. "Oh, for heaven's sake, Beatrice. If you spent half as much time minding your own business as you do inventing tales about me, this town would be a quieter place."

A few shoppers paused, items forgotten in their carts.

"You stole Harold from me!" Beatrice shrieked.

"I did no such thing. He left to join the army. He left us both." Melba wagged her finger.

The store manager, Oswald Chambers, hurried over, his apron flapping. "Ladies, please!" Oswald raised his hands. "Let's keep it civil, or take it outside. We're all neighbors here."

Melba and Beatrice glared at each other but quieted, muttering under their breaths as Oswald steered Melba back behind the soda fountain counter.

Beatrice, stomping as she walked, went down the produce aisle.

Georgia, curious and a little amused, sidled up to Oswald as he straightened a stack of soup cans.

"Oswald," She whispered. "Why do they always argue? What happened between them?" She'd heard rumors most of her life, but maybe Oswald knew more details.

He sighed, glanced over his shoulder, his gaze sweeping the area. "Those two?" He lowered his voice. "Used to be thick as thieves when they were young. Then Beatrice got it into her head that Melba stole her beau, Harold. Accused Melba of all sorts of things, some not too polite. The truth?" Oswald shrugged. "Only Harold would know, and he joined the army before anyone could sort it out. Never came back, as far as I know. So, the truth behind the accusations remains a mystery, leaving the rest of us to wonder." Oswald shook his head. "If those two would just sit and talk about what happened, maybe they could forgive one another."

Georgia nodded slowly, watching Melba and Beatrice shoot daggers at each other from opposite ends of the store. Some feuds, it seemed, never faded.

Thank goodness, she and Tanya never had a fight or a feud. But what would happen if she admitted the truth to Tanya?

Georgia whimpered, grabbed a cart, and hurried to get the items for the break room.

Clint drove the four-wheeler along the fence lining the back pasture.

The last evening with Georgia left him with a lingering sense of happiness. He kept replaying their conversation, her laughter, and the kisses they shared. Could last night be the start of something more between them? He hoped so.

He couldn't believe how much had changed since he returned to Garden Valley, and how Georgia had already become an important part of his life.

Once he finished his chores, he'd stop by Shaffer's and see if she would be open to having dinner again with him tonight at the new bistro in town.

But what if he was rushing things? What if the same thing happened with Georgia that happened with his ex-girlfriend?

Could he risk failing again?

Would God actually give him a second chance at love?

Trying to leave his doubts behind, Clint gunned the four-wheeler and raced across the property.

# *Chapter 13*

Time was up. She had to do this. Georgia hesitated. Why couldn't she keep pretending nothing happened? Was this really necessary? Everything turned out okay. Tanya and Blake married and were happy.

Then again, she didn't want to be like Melba and Beatrice. Georgia straightened her shoulders, stepped into the police station, and walked to her friend's desk. She wanted nothing to come between her friendship with Tanya.

Tanya looked up from her computer as Georgia entered her cubicle. "Hey, you're just in time. I'd love to get some feedback on the information I'm going to post on the police website."

Georgia sat on the edge of her chair. "What about?"

"ATV thefts." Tanya's gaze stayed on her computer. "Here's what I've written. Theft of ATVs is often difficult to trace because they are not subject to title requirements, which makes recovery efforts challenging. It is essential to keep a record of your ATV's serial number. Install tracking devices on your vehicles, and it is advisable to insure your equipment and avoid leaving it exposed on your property." Tanya glanced her way. "What do you think?"

They'd always been honest with each other. Well, almost always. "Kinda wordy," Georgia said with a flinch. "Why not just keep it simple? Keep a record of your serial number, insure your equipment, install a tracking device, and don't leave it out in the open."

Tanya gazed at her. "Short and simple?"

"Works best for me." Georgia nodded.

"I'll keep tweaking." Tanya tilted her head as she gazed at her. "What's up? What brings you by in the middle of the day?"

A two-way radio crackled, its static followed by the scratchy sound of someone sorting through files. A printer in the next cubicle whirred, breaking the silence.

Georgia, her nerves on edge, kept adjusting her purse strap. "I need to tell you something. About someone you dated a few years ago." She took a deep breath, let it out. "I've been carrying it with me for years. When you were dating Mark." She swallowed hard as the memories returned. "I let my insecurities get the better of me. He, uh, Mark, said some things to me."

Tanya leaned in, her jaw clenching and her eyes slightly narrowing. "What things?"

Georgia took a trembling breath. "Not bad things. Nice things. Mark said I was pretty, and he, uh, asked me to go to dinner with him. It was one of those times you were out of town. I'm so sorry. I went with him, and afterwards, he kissed me. I'm so sorry. I should've told you sooner."

Tanya leaned back in her chair, shook her head, and remained silent.

Tears streamed down Georgia's face, and she struggled to keep going. "I was feeling insecure, and he made me feel okay about myself, but afterwards I felt terrible. I shouldn't have gone with him. I shouldn't have let him kiss me." Georgia sobbed out the words. "And I should never have done that to my best friend. I'm so sorry. Please, please forgive me."

Her friend said nothing for a moment. "You've carried that for two years?"

Shaking with sobs, Georgia nodded.

Tanya blew out a breath. "I wish you had told me sooner."

"I'm so sorry. I felt like God had been nudging me to be

honest with you. I've asked for forgiveness from God many times, and I believe He has forgiven me." Georgia was rambling, but she couldn't stop. "I kept thinking I needed to talk to you, tell you what had happened, apologize, and ask for your forgiveness. I should have told you back then, but I was so afraid you would hate me."

"I would never hate you," Tanya whispered, her voice barely audible.

Georgia's lip trembled. "Really?"

"Really." With a sigh, Tanya rubbed her forehead. "I knew what happened. Mark wasn't great at keeping secrets. I think he wanted me to know that someone else thought he was a catch. He wasn't." Tanya came around her desk and sat in the chair next to Georgia. "Honestly, I'm not mad at you. I appreciate you telling me, but my breakup with Mark had nothing to do with you."

Georgia sucked in a sob. "I've felt guilty for so long— convinced I ruined everything. Not that I wanted you to keep dating him, but I thought the breakup was because of me."

"No, Mark made his own choices. I had already discovered he wasn't the faithful type. I should never have gone out with him. I've always been in love with Blake."

"You definitely chose the better man." Georgia hiccupped through her tears.

"That's for sure. And as for you, I'm glad you told me." Tanya squeezed Georgia's hand. "You don't have to carry that anymore."

"Thank you. That means more than you know."

"I wonder if God kept nudging you to apologize and ask for forgiveness, so that you didn't have to keep carrying what happened."

Georgia sucked in a breath. Could that be true? God had

already forgiven her. Tanya already knew and had forgiven her. But she hadn't forgiven herself. What was that statement Jesus made? *You will know the truth, and the truth will set you free.*

It was wrong of her to be with Mark, considering he was her best friend's boyfriend at the time.

Georgia took a deep breath and let it out. Even though she'd done the right thing by going to God for forgiveness, it wasn't until she apologized to her friend that she discovered the rest of the story – the rest of the truth. Freedom came with that realization.

For the first time in a long while, Georgia felt a lightness spread through her. She was forgiven by God and her friend.

The weight of carrying her betrayal against Tanya finally released, hit the floor with a crash, and scattered into nothingness.

# *Chapter 14*

Hoping to see Georgia, Clint stepped inside Shaffer's Outfitters. His boots echoed on the old wooden floor as he scanned the rows of fishing rods, camping equipment, backpacks, hiking boots, kayaks, and climbing gear.

Richard Shaffer, tall and straight-backed, restocked shelves with military precision. Behind the counter, Georgia's mom, Beth Shaffer, looked up, and her eyes lit with recognition. "Clint Briscoe! Well, it's been a while. What brings you in today?"

Clint offered a polite smile. "Hi, Mrs. Shaffer, Mr. Shaffer. I was hoping to see Georgia. Is she around?"

Richard set down a box of tackle supplies and studied Clint with a friendly but measured gaze. "She should be back soon."

Beth leaned on the counter. "It's good to have you back in Garden Valley, Clint. Are you enjoying living here?"

Clint nodded. "I am. I'm settling in, working on the farm."

"Glad to hear it." Richard gave an approving nod as he moved next to Beth and put his arm around her. "That land's been in your family a long time. Takes a steady hand to keep it going."

"I'm learning as I go. Still getting used to the early mornings."

"Early mornings, late nights, and a never-ending list of chores. That's farm life. You'll get used to it. Or at least, you'll get used to being tired."

Clint laughed. "I believe it." With the early mornings he was keeping, he went to bed earlier than at any other point in his life, yet he still felt tired.

"How's your grandfather?" Beth asked.

"He's doing well thanks to Janis Lucas's cinnamon rolls and good company.

"Mom's enjoying being with Wayne. And I hear you've been spending time with Georgia?" Beth gave a knowing smile.

Clint's ears heated. "We've caught up a little." He looked about, hoping to find Georgia. "I wanted to see if she's up for dinner tonight and maybe a walk."

"She went to see Tanya," Richard said, "but I'm sure she'll be back soon. Can I show you anything in the store while you wait?"

Clint glanced down at his worn, dusty boots. He did need something nicer. "I guess I could use another pair since working on the farm is taking a toll on these."

"Follow me, and I'll get you fixed up." Richard motioned toward the shoe section. "And by the way, welcome home."

While shopping for new boots, Clint found himself relaxing during the pleasant, surprisingly comfortable conversation with Georgia's parents.

Watching Richard and Beth's loving interaction made Clint long for a connection that went beyond the one he'd seen between his parents. He knew his mom and dad loved one another, but his dad was overbearing and demanding of his wife and sons.

Georgia's dad, Richard, was obviously a man's man, yet he had a tender side with Beth. And from what Clint remembered from earlier conversations with Georgia, she adored her dad. The only good quality of Clint's dad was his strong work ethic. The man demanded respect, whether he deserved it or not.

Clint shoved his feet into the new boots he was trying, then walked around to see how they fit. Not bad. He could replace his worn-out ones and have a spare to wear when he was off the farm.

Georgia had to focus not to break out in song as she headed back to work. She was blown away that Tanya had already known what happened, yet still offered forgiveness. Georgia took a deep, happy breath.

No wonder God kept nudging her to address what happened with her friend. The worry that had lingered in her thoughts was finally gone. She was free.

She opened the door to Shaffer's, stepped inside, and spotted Clint in the shoe section. The day just kept getting better and better. Georgia walked over to where he sat, trying on a pair of boots. "Buying some new ones?"

"Yeah. What do you think?" Clint held up one foot.

"Looks great. Do they fit okay?"

"Yeah," Clint rose to his feet and took a few steps. "They're comfortable. Fit better than any I've ever bought before."

"Dad knows his stuff," Georgia sent a grin toward her father.

"I'll take them." Clint kept on the new boots and put his old ones in the box.

As he made his purchase, he leaned toward Georgia. "I wanted to see if you're up for dinner after work. Thought maybe we could take a walk after?"

Georgia smiled. "I'd love to." She gave her parents a quick glance for approval. Dad gave her a slight smile and a simple nod.

Mom gave a subtle thumbs-up. "If you want to leave for the day, we have you covered."

Trying not to break into a happy dance, Georgia composed herself as she walked next to Clint as they made their way along the sidewalk.

The sun was shining, birds were singing, and a fluffy cloud shaped like a heart floated in the sky.

They entered the crowded bistro, and Georgia sat diagonally from Clint. As she slid into her seat, her hand traced the smooth grain of the wooden table, its warmth grounding her in the bustling space. The aroma of freshly brewed coffee mingled with the scent of simmering homemade soup, making her stomach grumble.

Georgia scanned the menu, mentally weighing the sandwiches, burgers, wraps, and vibrant seasonal salads. She looked at Clint, catching his soft smile. "What do you think?" She gestured to the list of signature dishes inspired by local ingredients.

"It all sounds good. Not a single liver product." He grinned and set the menu down. "I'll play it safe and try their bistro burger and fries. How about you?"

"I'm going to order the fiesta salad. Practical but spicy."

An amused gleam lit Clint's eyes. "Kind of like you, huh?"

Georgia gave him a curious look. "You see me as practical and spicy?"

"Sure. You're a hometown girl, but you're not satisfied with a mundane job. You want to be involved with some excitement."

She liked that thought. Practical, spicy, and exciting.

The waitress took their orders and left.

Clint leaned closer. "So, exactly why did you decide on being a private eye?"

Georgia straightened. "It all began with Aloysius. I was sure a hawk had killed him."

He blinked, his eyes widening, before he stared at her, and

then a grin spread across his face. "That's right. He was your hamster. If I remember correctly, based on what you shared one summer, his name was Aloysius P. Higginbotham."

Surprised he remembered, she smiled. "Yes, and that's what started my quest to solve mysteries. I love searching for clues." She glanced at him. "What did you want to be when you grew up?"

For a fleeting second, a shadow clouded Clint's eyes, but then his smile returned, though it wasn't as bright. "I wanted to be taller, faster, and stronger."

She swallowed hard, her heart aching at the pain she saw in his eyes. "I think you're perfect just as you are." Georgia extended her hand towards him, her palm open, hoping for the warmth of his touch.

Clint clasped her fingers in his. "Thank you."

"I'm not just saying that." She couldn't believe he was insecure. How could he not see what a wonderful guy he was?

The waitress delivered their order, and Georgia reluctantly slid her hand from Clint's.

He placed a napkin on his lap, then gazed her way. "So, do you pray in public?"

Georgia grinned. "Yes, and I'd love to, since today has been an incredible day."

"Sounds interesting. Care to share?"

"Tell you what, I'll bless the food and then we can talk." Georgia leaned close to Clint and said a quick prayer, thanking God for the blessings He had given and asking God to bless Clint.

When she opened her eyes, he pressed his forehead against hers. "Thank you."

"You're welcome." His lips were so close and so tempting.

Someone cleared their throat close to their table.

Georgia glanced up.

The police chief gazed down at them with a wide smile. "Hope you both enjoy your meal." He chuckled and walked away.

Embarrassed heat ran up Georgia's back. She picked up her fork and started eating. If the Chief hadn't been here, she probably would have kissed Clint, right here in view of everyone.

"Shame we were interrupted," Clint said. The teasing in his eyes sparked her grin.

"Yes, it is a shame."

"I think after dinner maybe we could continue our discussion somewhere more private." His gaze went from her eyes to her lips.

Her mouth twitched in a happy response. "I think that's a wonderful idea."

## *Chapter 15*

Georgia strolled next to Clint along the path behind her cabin. The evening sun dipped behind the Tennessee hills, painting the sky a peachy and orange hue. They walked in comfortable silence, the distant crickets chirping their evening song.

"I'm grateful I came back." Clint reached for her hand, his thumb tracing slow circles on her skin. "I didn't realize how much I missed this place—or you."

Georgia's breath caught, and she squeezed his fingers. "I'm glad you're here, too."

"You mentioned earlier you were having an incredible day. Care to share?"

She bumped Clint's shoulder. "Besides being with you. I had a great conversation with Tanya."

"I thought you were best friends. Aren't most of your conversations good?"

"This one was different." Georgia took a deep breath. "Have you ever done something you regret?"

He gave her a curious look. "Yes. Haven't most people?"

Georgia looked down, gathering her courage. "Two years ago, I did something I shouldn't have and felt guilty ever since. I finally apologized to Tanya."

A squirrel scampered out in front of them, paused to scold them with a flurry of chirps, and then vanished up a tree.

Clint gently squeezed her hand. "You made a mistake, but you owned up to it. That takes courage."

"Took me long enough." Georgia scuffed her shoe on the

dirt trail. "The interesting part was that Tanya already knew, and she'd forgiven me even before I could say I was sorry. I figured out that God's gentle nudges to ask her for forgiveness cleared the air and cleared my thoughts, and I can finally stop worrying about what happened."

Clint held a branch blocking the trail, allowing her to duck beneath it. "Interesting. The other day, when I was talking with Pops, he said something that stuck with me. He said I needed to leave behind the useless regret and morbid looking back."

Georgia stopped and stared at him. "Useless regret and morbid looking back. Wow. That's great advice."

"Yeah, it is. I need to remember to give things to God, ask for forgiveness if needed, then let them go, and stop looking back."

Could she do that? Stop worrying about the past? "That's easier said than done sometimes, isn't it?"

"Yeah, it isn't always easy." Clint took her hand, and together they continued on the winding trail.

"I haven't really talked much about what happened with my ex," He spoke, his voice low and thoughtful. "Sometimes I wonder if I should just leave it in the past, but I don't want there to be secrets between us."

Georgia looked up at him. "You don't need to tell me anything until you're comfortable."

Clint nodded, taking a steadying breath. "We were together for a long time. I thought she was the one. I even planned a big proposal. Rented a venue, invited friends and family, the whole nine yards." He gave a soft scoff. "Turns out, she'd been seeing my best friend behind my back. The night I proposed, she left with him. They got married two weeks later."

Georgia sucked in a breath. She couldn't imagine someone doing that to her sweet, handsome friend. "Clint, I'm so sorry.

That must have been devastating."

"It was. I felt like a fool. I didn't get much support from my family, other than my mom. My dad and brothers just saw it as another one of my failures. That's part of the reason I left Nashville to come here. I needed to start over somewhere I could breathe."

"You're not a failure, Clint. What happened wasn't your fault. You trusted and cared for someone. That's not a weakness. Even if she was a no-good, wicked woman." Georgia growled.

Clint gave her a funny look, raising one eyebrow in amusement. "Thanks. Nice to know you'd stand up for me."

She rested her head on his shoulder, content. "No more useless regret and morbid looking back."

"I second that motion." He put his arm around her. "Being here with you feels like a second chance."

"Maybe a new beginning."

He leaned down and kissed her. "Second chance with a new beginning sounds good to me."

She returned his kiss with a smile, the soft brush of his lips sending shivers down her spine.

They stood together in the moonlit clearing. All was right with the world until Georgia heard the kamikaze sound of a mosquito buzzing near her ear.

She yelped and swatted at the blood-sucking parasite. "They're after me."

"What's wrong?"

"Don't you remember how bugs are attracted to me?"

Clint shook his head. "I forgot since they didn't seem to bother you on our last walk."

"That's because it was windy enough to blow them away." Georgia swatted at a mosquito that landed on her bare arm. "They're making up for lost time tonight."

A low, guttural growl vibrated through the night air, curling out from the shadows and prickling the hairs on Georgia's arms. The sound was so raw, so close, it seemed to sink beneath her skin.

Clint shoved her behind him, his hand trembling just enough for her to notice.

Georgia's heart hammered against her ribs as she peeked over his shoulder, her breath coming in short bursts. "That's... disturbing," she whispered, her voice barely more than a shiver.

He took a cautious step back, pulling her with him, his grip tightening around her hand. "Come on, let's get you back home." His words were steady, but she could hear the strain in them.

They bobbed and weaved through the trees, branches clawing at their clothes.

Georgia's sneakers slipped on the mossy trail, and she wished she'd worn rollerblades, or anything that would make her faster.

A deer exploded from the underbrush in front of them, its hooves thudding against the ground. Georgia bit back a scream, her throat tight, as the animal's white tail flashed and vanished into the deep, swallowing shadows.

They kept running until they reached her cabin. As soon as they were inside, Clint shut and locked the door.

Gasping for air, the echo of the growl still thrumming in Georgia's chest, she clung to Clint. "What was that?"

He held her close. "Not a clue, but I wasn't going to wait around to find out. Sounded like a mountain lion or some other big cat."

She stayed snuggled in his arms, listening to his rapid heartbeat. "I think we beat a land speed record."

"We got away from whatever that was, but did we outrun the bloodsuckers?"

Georgia scratched at the angry red welts blooming on her arm, wincing as the sting left a trail of heat. "All but a few. I think they left me a souvenir or two."

Clint grinned as he looked down at her. "If you weren't so sweet, the bugs wouldn't bother you."

Georgia wrinkled her nose, peering at him with mock indignation. "I'm not sure being irresistible to bugs is the superpower I want. Maybe I need to develop a taste for garlic or wear a suit of armor."

She swatted at another persistent mosquito buzzing near her ear that must have followed her inside. "I guess I'll have to add mosquito magnet to my resume. Want to be my official bug bodyguard?"

He tilted her chin, brushing away a stray hair that clung to her cheek. "Just say the word, and I'm yours."

Georgia's heart fluttered with the wonderful thought of Clint being hers. "Well, keep your bug bodyguard badge handy. The way critters like me, it would be a long-term assignment."

"Long-term, huh?" Clint's eyebrows raise with his smile. "If my duties come with kisses, I'm your man." His lips met hers in a soft, lingering kiss. "Just as I thought. Sweet with a hint of spice."

Her legs turned weak, and a soft, dreamy sigh slipped from her lips. "You, Mr. Briscoe, are the best."

A mournful yowling came from outside, sending a shiver up Georgia's spine.

Clint's eyes widened, and his gaze darted around her cabin. "Do you have a weapon? Baseball bat?"

"I have a gun, but I'm not sure we should shoot anything. And even if I had a bat, I don't think I'd want you to go outside." Georgia flicked on the porch light, then tiptoed to the window.

She parted the curtains and peered out. At the sight of her

furry visitor, laughter bubbled up. "It's Captain Jack."

Clint hurried over. "The pirate?"

"No, silly. It's the cat that hangs out on our property."

"A cat? How big is he?" Clint squinted through the glass. "Seriously? Okay, he is pretty big. But was he the one making that noise?"

"I don't know if that was him in the woods, but it looks like he bought me something." Georgia eased open the door.

Captain Jack, tail held high and fur puffed out like a proud lion, strutted toward her and dropped a limp, scaly, dead snake at her feet.

Georgia shuddered but pasted on a smile. "Thank you, Captain Jack."

The cat answered with a throaty meow before turning to Clint and letting out a rumbling, deep growl.

She laughed. "Oh my goodness, I think he's jealous."

"Hey, buddy." Clint crouched to stroke the cat's thick fur.

Captain Jack jerked away, flicked his tail, shot Clint a look of pure feline disdain, and stalked away.

"Great." Clint's shoulders slumped. "My competition for your affection is a furry, four-legged pirate."

Georgia giggled, tugging him back inside.

## *Chapter 16*

The next morning, Georgia sat at her office desk and entered the man's name for a background check for SAU Tech.

With a contented sigh, she leaned back, recalling Clint's sweet kisses and the warmth of his embrace from the night before. Plus, the fun with Captain Jack had been hilarious. She hadn't had that much fun since, well, forever.

She'd had a crush on Clint since the summer they'd first met. And now they were together. Or at least she thought they were together since he'd agreed to be her bug bodyguard.

The background check results finished loading, and Georgia's eyes widened. A red flag appeared on the screen, a detail that didn't match the friendly face in the job candidate's photo.

She leaned in, squinting at the monitor. "Looks like this case just got a lot more interesting. Now, just what are you hiding?"

Georgia searched through social media looking for anything matching the man's name and description. There were discrepancies between his resume, the information he provided on various job platforms, and the addresses he listed. Why people weren't more careful about what they posted never ceased to amaze her.

Just who was that man, and why did he want to work in accounting for the company? She picked up her phone and dialed her contact at SAU Tech, explaining what she'd found.

When the call finished, Georgia decided she needed to

celebrate saving the company from the dishonest man, and a root beer float would be the perfect way to do so.

Georgia bounded down the stairs, her sandals thudding softly against the worn wooden steps. The faint scent of leather filled the air as she stepped onto the sales floor, where her mom stood in the shoe section, carefully arranging the latest boot shipment on the shelves.

"Hi, Mom. I'm heading to the general store. Do you need anything?"

Her mom glanced up and smiled. "Would you mind picking up some creamer for my coffee?"

"You betcha."

"So how was your date last night?"

At the thought of her wonderful evening with Clint, Georgia smiled and scrunched up her shoulders. "It was great."

Her mom grinned. "I can tell."

"Captain Jack scared us both. He was doing the weirdest yowl, growling thing that made my hair stand on end. I think he's jealous of Clint."

"Cats can be territorial. He's had you all to himself for years."

Georgia ran her hand along the wooden shelf. "Well, I hope he accepts Clint because I'm hoping he's around for a long time."

"You getting together again this evening?"

"I'm not sure. Clint said he would call." Or at least she hoped so.

Her mom paused, a knowing look in her eyes as she set a pair of boots neatly on the shelf. "He'd be a fool not to."

Georgia lingered for a moment, watching her mom fuss with a stubborn price tag.

She said goodbye to her mom, who offered a quick wave before turning her attention back to arranging boots.

With a bounce in her step, Georgia crossed the sunlit street, the morning air buzzing with the familiar sounds of her small town.

The bell above the general store door chimed as she walked in, and she made her way straight to the counter, choosing her favorite worn red vinyl stool. The seat gave a faint squeak beneath her as she settled in, and she rested her elbows on the linoleum surface.

Behind the counter, Melba wiped her hands on a small towel before tossing it over her shoulder, giving Georgia a welcoming grin. "You having the usual?"

Georgia nodded, "Yes, please."

Melba reached for a tall glass and raised a playful eyebrow. "You really should try something new. Let me fix you a Dr Pepper with a shot of vanilla. Best thing ever, I promise."

Georgia smiled, shaking her head. "Thanks, but I'll stick to my usual."

"No guts, no glory." Melba expertly scooped the ice cream and poured in the root beer, her movements practiced and precise, having spent years behind the counter. Finished, she slid the float in front of Georgia, the frosty glass fogging in the warm air. "So, any ongoing investigations?"

Georgia took a long, satisfying sip, letting the sweet, cold drink bubble against her tongue. She set the glass down and shrugged. "Nothing much."

Melba leaned in, the corners of her eyes crinkling with amusement. "I heard you had a run-in with a drop-in lizard."

Georgia tried to muster an innocent look, her lips quirking as she feigned surprise. "Would you believe he was a four-foot iguana?"

"Nope. Not even close." Melba chuckled and turned to tend to the next customer.

Taking a sip of her drink, Georgia gazed up at the mirror behind the counter. In the reflection, she noticed Clint near the candy aisle, deep in conversation with an attractive woman whose laughter rang clear and easy across the shop.

Georgia's heart squeezed. The woman was everything Georgia wasn't—effortlessly stylish, her dark, glossy hair catching the afternoon light, her smile wide and sure. Clint grinned in response, looking relaxed and animated. Georgia's insecurities pounced, unbidden and relentless.

Of course, her first real crush would crush her heart. She tore her gaze away, focusing hard on the fizzing bubbles and melting ice cream, hoping the sting in her chest would fade.

Georgia's mind raced through every moment they'd shared, the jokes, the warmth, the sweet kisses, and wondered if she'd fooled herself into thinking she could ever be enough.

She set down the float, unfinished, and pressed her palm to her forehead, trying not to let disappointment show on her face while the voices behind her mingled with the clinks of soda glasses.

Just her luck. She'd finally let herself hope, and already, it seemed, hope was slipping away. Shoving off her seat, Georgia hurried back to work.

Clint couldn't believe he'd run into the physical therapist who helped Pops. She'd always treated his grandfather with respect, even sharing stories about her young kid's sticky-fingered mischief, the way they'd chase each other through the kitchen, leaving a trail of giggles and cookie crumbs.

Perhaps someday he'd have a happy family, and he hoped that family started with Georgia Shaffer. After last night, things looked very promising.

As the therapist said her goodbyes and headed out the door, Clint glimpsed Georgia's retreating back. As if upset, her shoulders were tense, her steps brisk.

He needed to make sure she was okay. Clint hurried to complete his shopping and rushed to his truck to unload the groceries. Just as he finished, his cell rang.

Clint answered. He was needed back at the farm. With a deep sigh, he glanced across the street toward Shaffer's. He'd have to check on Georgia later.

# *Chapter 17*

**Wh**y was Clint talking with that attractive woman? Who was she? An old girlfriend? Someone new in town?

Georgia hurried to her office and plopped into her desk chair. She tried to focus on her work, but her mind kept replaying the image of Clint laughing with the attractive woman in the general store. The memory gnawed at her, stirring up old insecurities she thought she'd left behind.

A gentle knock at the door broke her reverie. She looked up to see her mom standing in the doorway.

"Are you okay?"

Georgia ran her fingers through her hair, feeling the tangles catch and pull—a physical echo of her tangled thoughts. "No, and yes. Oh, I don't know."

Her mom came in and sat across from her. "Want to talk about it?"

"I saw Clint talking to an attractive woman."

"Okay."

Georgia sighed. "Maybe it wasn't a big deal, maybe she was a family friend, but I started worrying maybe that she was an old girlfriend or someone he's interested in. He looked so happy with her."

"You're letting the insecurities attack again, aren't you?"

"Yes, and I hate it. Why can't I be confident? The only thing I'm confident about is that I'm a loser and will probably lose the man I care about."

Her mom leaned toward her, her expression kind. "Perhaps it's because you don't believe the beautiful, kind, loving, sweet, fun woman that you are."

"I wish." Georgia scoffed. Maybe she was okay looking and an okay person, but beautiful? Not so much.

"Do you think that by being so focused on yourself, you could be blind to what's really going on?"

"What do you mean?"

Her mom sighed. "When I was a teenager, I was very self-conscious."

"You?" Georgia couldn't imagine her gorgeous mom ever being insecure. Even in early photos, her mom was beautiful.

"I kept worrying about how I looked. And one day I was talking with a girl in my high school geology class, and she looked at me and said, 'You are so stuck up!'"

Georgia shook her head. "What? Why would she say that?"

"That was my response. But then she said When I kept fixating on myself, how I thought I looked and acted, I was self-absorbed."

"Ouch. I haven't ever looked at it that way."

"God created each of us with distinct features, from our varying skin tones to diverse national backgrounds. We should aim to be the best person we can be, but not be so self-obsessed that we lose sight of everything else."

Was she doing that? Georgia's fingers gently brushed over the surface of her birthmark. Her insecurities had cast a shadow over her college years, strained friendships, and were now threatening her relationship with Clint.

"I'm sure there's a reasonable explanation about Clint and the woman," her mom said. "Please don't let your insecure thoughts take you somewhere you shouldn't go. And, honey, even if there was another woman, you need to remember who you truly are. You are a beautiful, kind, loving, sweet, fun woman. I'm not just saying that because I'm your mother. It's true."

"Would you say that if I were still a mutant like I was in middle school?"

Her mom grinned. "I could honestly say those statements because true beauty doesn't come from an outward appearance. The most beautiful woman I've ever known was your great-grandmother. Outwardly, she was plain, but she had a beautiful heart that radiated her inward attraction. And that kind of beauty is ageless."

Pops had told him where to find Daisy. The notoriously cranky cow pawed the ground, her tail swishing with irritation. Daisy had gotten herself wedged against a tree and the fence, bellowing and tossing her head at anyone who dared approach.

"Easy, girl." Clint kept talking in a low, soothing voice. With steady movements, he sidestepped her lunges. Once in position in front of her, he was able to push the fence post with just enough force to give her room to get free.

With a joyful kick of her hoofs, Daisy trotted off into the green pasture, strutting like she hadn't been trapped at all.

Clint grinned and shook his head. He'd made peace with Daisy. Now, he needed to find out what was bothering Georgia.

He drove back to town and stepped inside Shaffer's Outfitters.

Georgia's parents were busy with customers, so he waited by checking out the wall of fishing rods. Maybe he'd look at getting one for Pops next birthday.

Beth finished with her customer, then walked to where

Clint stood. "Hi, you here to see Georgia?"

"Yeah, is she in?"

"She's upstairs in her office." She motioned with her hand, directing him toward the back. "Take the stairs, and her office is the first one on the left."

Clint thanked her, hurried up the stairs, and peeked in Georgia's office, where she sat at her desk, her eyes fixed on the computer screen.

"Hey." Clint knocked on the doorframe. "Got a minute?"

She looked up, her expression guarded, a flicker of vulnerability in her eyes. "Hi, Clint."

He stepped inside and crossed to her desk. "I saw you earlier, and you looked upset. Is everything okay?"

Georgia shook her head, but he could tell something was bothering her.

Had something happened at the store? Then it hit him. Had she seen him talking to Mrs. Patterson? But why would that upset Georgia? Was she worried he was seeing other women? His last girlfriend couldn't have cared less, which was another clue that she hadn't been the right one for him.

Clint sat across from Georgia. "I'm sorry I missed you earlier. I was talking with Pop's physical therapist, Mrs. Patterson. She was a great help after his surgery. She loves sharing about her mischievous little kids."

Georgia's gaze met his, and a look of relief crossed her face.

So, she had been worried.

"Hey, you don't have to worry about me, or about us." He extended his hand toward her. "I'm your official bug buster, remember?"

"Thank you," she said, a small smile gracing her lips as she laid her hand in his.

"If you'd like, we could make it even more official." Clint

tried to find a way to make his offer sound more sophisticated and adult, but couldn't come up with anything beyond the simple statement. "Want to be my girlfriend?"

Georgia's smile widened, and she squeezed his hand. "I'd really like that."

"Good. Because I'm not going anywhere." Clint rose to his feet, came around to where she was sitting, pulled her to her feet, and gave her a kiss to seal the deal.

Clint held Georgia tight, hoping and praying she wouldn't break his already damaged heart.

## *Chapter 18*

Georgia rushed inside her cabin, attempting to tidy up before Clint arrived. He had called to let her know he was picking up a pizza from the Italian restaurant for their dinner. She was still amazed that they were now officially a couple.

Earlier today, when he left the store, she let her mom know she was dating Clint, then called both her grandmother and Tanya. Given how excited they all were, it was as though he'd proposed marriage.

The thought made Georgia feel dizzy with hope. Could something that wonderful ever happen? She gazed at the ceiling, silently wishing for God's approval. Still, she reminded herself to take things one day at a time and focus on enjoying her moments with Clint.

Once the family room was clean and ready, she set the table, arranging plates, silverware, and glasses. Finished with her preparations, Georgia crossed to her front window and peered out. The evening sun cast long shadows as it dipped low, painting the clouds with a soft peach hue.

She took a deep breath. Could life get any better?

In the meadow, her grandmother's white farmhouse seemed to glow, its windows reflecting the evening light. What would happen if her grandmother got together with Clint's grandad? Where would they live?

The thoughts swirled around in Georgia's head, and although she would be thrilled if the older couple's relationship progressed to marriage, how would they ever give up their own land?

Then the thought hit her. What would happen if she and Clint got married? Where would they live? Would he want to stay in her cabin? If not, what would happen to her beloved family's property?

Georgia shook her head, trying to clear her thoughts. Why was she worrying about any of those things? She had today, right now, and she needed to enjoy the moment.

The gravel drive crunched under Clint's pickup as it made its way toward her cabin. He exited the vehicle, holding the pizza aloft like a waiter presenting a meal to a customer.

She opened the door just as he reached the top of the wooden steps.

Clint grinned. "Pizza delivery." With a flourish, he bowed and held out the box.

"Come in, kind sir." The aroma of pizza filled the air as she led him inside.

Georgia poured two glasses of iced tea as they settled across from one another at her kitchen table, the pizza steaming between them.

Without even asking, Clint took her hand in his, then said a sweet prayer, asking God to bless the food and their relationship.

After he finished, Georgia, feeling all sorts of warm and wonderful emotions, squeezed his fingers. "Thank you."

"My pleasure." Clint took a generous first bite, obviously savoring the food. "So," he began after swallowing, "Pops and Janis were together at Pops' place, sitting on the porch, laughing over old stories. Looked like they were having a really good time."

"They sure are spending lots of time together, aren't they?"

He nodded. "Their favorite topic tonight was Pops' first

tractor. Janis was teasing him about how he named it after a movie star." Clint grinned, shaking his head. "Honestly, it's nice seeing Pops so happy. Between losing my grandmother and his health issues, he's had a rough couple of years. Janis brings out his old spark."

Georgia rested her hand on Clint's. "I'm glad. She's been happier than I've seen her since Grumps passed. It's wonderful to think that they might have a second chance at love."

His grin widened. "I'm all for second chances."

"Me too."

They ate in gentle, companionable silence until Georgie remembered her reaction to seeing Clint with the other woman.

Georgia's heart thudded in her chest as she searched for the right words. She stole glances at Clint, her hands fidgeting with her glass.

Finally, she summoned her courage. "I'm really sorry for how I acted when I saw you talking with Mrs. Paterson." Her cheeks heated with old, familiar embarrassment as she met his gaze. "Most of my life, I've felt like the awkward kid, always on the outside looking in." Georgia willed her hands to remain still, away from her birthmark. "I guess sometimes those old fears sneak up and make me see things that aren't really there."

Clint's head tilted as though surprised. "That's not who you are. You're wonderful, beautiful, smart, and fun." He let out a slow breath. "But I get what you're saying. My dad always wanted me to be taller, faster, and stronger. My brothers got all the good genes. I spent years thinking I was just the leftover Briscoe."

"You? But you're kind, smart, handsome, and—" She hesitated, then laughed. "And you smell good, even after working on the farm."

Clint grinned, but his eyes were serious. "Doesn't mean I

don't doubt myself. After what happened with my ex-girlfriend, I started wondering if I was just easy to leave behind."

Georgia's heart squeezed. The pain in Clint's voice stirred something tender and protective deep inside her. "I'm so sorry." She reached her hand toward his. "I would never leave you behind."

Clint's fingers wrapped around hers. He held on as if she were a lifeline, his thumb gently tracing the back of her hand.

"Thanks," he murmured. "You're not getting rid of me." He gazed at her, really gazed, and Georgia saw it then: the vulnerability behind his playful smiles, the loneliness he'd carried, not so different from hers.

She realized she wasn't the only one who had ever felt like an outsider or struggled with doubts that whispered she didn't belong. For the first time in a long while, she didn't feel so alone.

"I guess we're both a little broken," he said softly. "But maybe that's okay. Maybe being broken means we fit together better."

As a wide, genuine grin spread across Clint's face, lighting up his eyes, Georgia's own smile bloomed to match.

Maybe their flaws didn't make them unlovable, but made them perfectly suited, the jagged edges lining up just right. At the thought, a joyful, fluttering warmth rushed through her, a happiness that shimmered along her spine and made her feel light, hopeful, whole.

Yet a question remained, lingering at the edge of her heart—a question she needed to ask, though it made her feel exposed and vulnerable. Georgia hesitated, the words catching in her throat, but the need for honesty pressed her forward. "What do you think about my birthmark?" The tremor in her voice betrayed her uncertainty; she wanted to pretend it didn't matter, yet it mattered more than she could admit.

Clint's gaze softened as he studied her face. He rose to his feet and came toward her, kneeling next to her. His thumb gently brushed her cheek and traced a path down her neck, lingering on her birthmark, as if to say he saw every part of her.

He smiled—a slow, earnest smile that radiated warmth and acceptance. "That's not a birthmark, that's a God kiss," he said, voice filled with gentle conviction. "You know it looks like a heart, don't you?"

Georgia blinked, surprised by the tenderness in his answer and the way he transformed what she'd always regarded as a flaw into something beautiful.

A rush of emotion tightened her chest—relief, gratitude, hope—all mingling together as she realized he saw past her insecurities.

Her lip trembled with emotion, but her heart felt lighter, her worries eased by the sincerity in Clint's eyes. "You're pretty good at this romantic stuff, Mr. Briscoe," she said, her voice brighter, a laugh tucked beneath her words.

He shrugged, a playful glint dancing in his eyes as if determined to chase away any lingering sadness. "I still have lots to learn. Want to be my teacher?"

Heat ran up her back as she stared into his chocolate-brown eyes. "I'm sure we can stumble along together. So, no more morbid looking back and useless regret, right?"

"That's right. We're moving forward. Together." He pulled her to her feet.

As he kissed her long, sweet, and slow, Georgia's heart swelled with something brave and new.

*Chapter 19*

Georgia stood by her office window, watching the leaves swirl in the crisp fall afternoon air. The heart of downtown Garden Valley shimmered with vibrant fall hues as crimson, amber, and gold leaves cartwheeled down the sidewalk.

She felt as happy as those skipping leaves and still couldn't believe she and Clint had been officially dating for two months, three weeks, and one day. Not that she was counting. Much.

Her phone rang, jolting her from her daydream. Melba's voice burst through, breathless and dramatic as ever. "Georgia, come quick! There's been a disturbance at the old train depot. Folks heard a whistle blowing at midnight, but the tracks haven't seen a train in years!"

Her curiosity piqued, Georgia grabbed her notebook and keys. "On my way." She placed a quick call to Tanya, then hurried down the stairs.

Georgia stopped. Why did Melba call her? And if a whistle blew at midnight, why was Melba so worried now, like it had just happened? It was strange since the train depot and tracks had been unused for decades.

After a quick explanation to her parents, Georgia stepped outside into the nippy air, her boots crunching over a patchwork of leaves. She breathed deep of the spicy-sweet scent of autumn, the rich scent of cinnamon and fresh pastry from the bakery, and a mingling of distant woodsmoke.

At the depot, a small crowd clustered together, voices bubbling with excitement and worry, steam curling from coffee cups clutched in mittened hands.

Tanya's police car rolled into the lot. She hopped out and closed the door behind her. "Looks like the whole town's in an uproar," she said with an exaggerated eye roll.

Georgia moved close to her friend. "I have no idea why everyone is so excited about a train whistle."

Her friend chuckled. "You know as well as I do, in Garden Valley, anything could happen."

Melba, Beatrice, and others chattered over each other, their words tumbling like the swirling leaves. Melba insisted she'd heard the whistle clear as a bell, while Beatrice argued it must've been nothing more than the wind moaning through the depot's broken windows.

"Okay, people. I'll go check the office," Tanya announced.

"I'll check around outside." Georgia circled the perimeter, noting footprints pressed into the soft dirt smaller than her own.

A small scrap of red fabric fluttered on a rusty nail, its color stark against the weathered gray boards. Georgia examined the piece of vaguely familiar cloth. It looked like a scarf she'd seen someone wearing recently. But who?

Tanya strode back, her breath visible in the chilly air. "Looks like someone's recently oiled the whistle."

"Strange. Why would they do that?" Georgia held up the cloth. "Someone's definitely been here."

"Probably just a prank," Tanya said.

"It's a midnight cry," a man suggested.

"Or maybe someone's trying to send a message." Melba piped up.

"That's ridiculous," Beatrice said with a look of disgust. "What kind of message would a train whistle send? I think it means something scary and terrible."

"It was Bigfoot!" Mr. Grady bellowed, his voice echoing

from his barbershop across the street and sending a ripple of laughter through the crowd.

As Tanya questioned the townsfolk, Georgia listened, the air buzzing with speculation. One man mentioned glimpsing a shadowy figure slinking near the depot the previous night.

Melba recalled hearing faint laughter mingled with the whistle, and Beatrice sheepishly admitted she'd seen Mr. Grady's dog nosing around. However, Beatrice doubted even a clever dog could manage a midnight whistle.

Moving away from the crowd, Tanya and Georgia pieced together the clues. The footprints were too small for an adult, and the cloth matched the scarf worn by Tommy, the local boy known for his practical jokes.

They found Tommy at the general store, sheepish but grinning. "I just wanted to see if anyone still listened for the trains. I oiled the whistle and blew it at midnight. Didn't mean to scare anyone." His words didn't match the mischievous glint in his eyes.

Tanya knelt to Tommy's level, her eyes twinkling with a mixture of sternness and humor. She held out a slip of paper, her voice firm. "Tommy, I'm officially issuing you a warning for midnight mischief. No more whistleblowing at odd hours."

Tommy's shoulders slumped as he nodded and took the ticket. However, a grin tugging at his lips betrayed his amusement as he examined the paper.

As he left the store. Georgia nudged Tanya. "Did you actually write him a ticket?"

"Not exactly. It's from my stash of pretend warning slips for things that aren't real police business. I bet Tommy's going to show it off to everyone at school tomorrow."

Georgia chuckled. "You'd better watch out. There might be a rash of mischief around town in the near future."

"You're probably right." Tanya sighed and nodded. "But if that's the only problem we have in town, I'll be grateful."

They walked out of the store together and stood on the sidewalk. Streetlights flickered on, casting warm pools of light onto the pavement.

As downtown shops began to close for the day, Rosie's and other restaurants were already filling up with customers.

Tanya shot her a sly smile. "Got a date tonight with your boyfriend?"

"Yep! We're having dinner at Rosie's."

"Yummy. I love Mexican food."

"I can't wait." The promise of spicy goodness and spending time with Clint made Georgia scrunch up her shoulders in happiness. "I'm overdue for some salsa. I'm going to load up on fajitas and have way too many bowls of salsa. Afterward, Clint's coming back to the cabin for drinks. Well, tea for me, coffee for him."

"You two really know how to party," Tanya teased.

"Clint really is wonderful."

"You realize you're both hopelessly infatuated, right?"

"Like you and Blake—totally head over heels."

Tanya laughed. "Isn't it the best feeling?"

Georgia gave her friend a high-five, their hands meeting with a satisfying clap in the cool air. "Absolutely."

Later that evening, walking beside Clint, Georgia stepped into Rosie's restaurant. The warmth of the restaurant wrapped around her like a cheerful hug. The walls glowed with color, every inch decorated with vibrant artwork, hand-painted tiles from Old Mexico, woven blankets draped over rustic pottery, and vintage sombreros perched at jaunty angles. The air smelled of cumin and chiles, and the subtle sounds of upbeat mariachi music drifted under the buzz of conversation.

A smiling hostess guided them to a cozy wooden booth tucked beneath a wrought-iron lantern.

Clint settled across from Georgia. "You know we ate here last week."

"Yes, I know. But you can't ever have too much salsa."

He grinned as he surveyed the menu. "Are you having your usual?"

"Of course. Chicken fajitas are a combination of protein, vegetables, and a healthy dash of yum."

Clint chuckled. "Well, everyone needs their daily dose of yum."

An attractive waitress with long brown hair and striking gray eyes stood next to their table. "Hi, I'm Sarah. Welcome to Rosie's. What can I get you to drink this evening?"

"Hi, Sarah. I think we're ready to order," Clint said, flashing a friendly grin and looking at Georgia for confirmation.

While placing their order, Georgia noticed that Sarah's voice and gestures reminded her of a college friend who'd experienced a tough childhood.

Sarah moved to another table, her smile flickering as she greeted an older couple. The polite smile and scribbled notes couldn't hide the sadness that flickered in Sarah's eyes before she turned away.

As Sarah moved on to the next table, Georgia reflected on her own reaction to Clint's easy friendliness and Sarah's striking presence. It wasn't long ago that she would have been jealous and insecure. But tonight, Georgia felt a quiet pride welling up inside her. She was growing beyond her insecurities. There was no need to compare herself or to worry about being overlooked. She could simply appreciate Sarah for who she was, seeing the subtle sadness in her eyes and wishing kindness for a fellow newcomer.

Georgia leaned toward Clint, lowering her voice. "Lots of new people in town."

Clint nodded and looked around at the bustling restaurant. "Yeah, Garden Valley keeps growing. SAU Tech's expansion brings more people into different areas, from professionals to trades. Just last week, I met a couple of new welders and a nurse at the coffee shop."

"I still have mixed emotions about the town's growth," Georgia said. "I'm grateful for the positive changes, but I hope it doesn't get too big. I like the personality of our little town."

Clint nodded, his eyes thoughtful. "It's hard to know what's next. Progress is good, but I guess we all want the things we love to stay the same, too."

Georgia glanced again at Sarah, who was now refilling water glasses for a large family. Hopefully, she would find that in Garden Valley, no one stayed a stranger for long.

Back at her cabin, Georgia carried her cup of hot tea out onto her front porch. She reached for the soft blue blanket she kept draped over her favorite rocker.

Her hand met only empty wood. She frowned, scanning the porch. She checked the railing, even under the flowerpots. No blanket.

Clint emerged from the cabin, coffee mug in hand. "Lose something?"

"My porch blanket's gone. I know it was here last night."

"Maybe the wind carried it off. Or maybe it's another Garden Valley mystery." His eyebrows danced with a mischievous tilt.

"Help me look for clues to what happened. I like that blanket."

A flash of fur darted across the yard and stopped. Captain Jack glanced in their direction, then slunk past, something blue trailing behind him.

Clint pointed. "Isn't that—?"

Georgia gasped. "Captain Jack! He's got my blanket!"

They put down their cups, then hurried after the cat, who paused again long enough to shoot Clint a look of pure disgust before disappearing into the brush. "Captain Jack! Come back here!" Georgia called.

They found him next to her woodpile, curled up on a nest of blue fleece, purring loudly.

Trying not to laugh, Georgia knelt by the big cat. "Jack, why did you take my blanket?"

Clint crouched beside her. "Maybe he's jealous since we're spending time together."

Georgia stroked the cat's head. "Is that it, buddy? Are you mad I'm dating Clint?"

Captain Jack responded by glaring at Clint, followed by a rumbling growl and a possessive paw on the blanket.

Clint chuckled. "Looks like I've got competition."

Georgia scooped up the stubborn cat and blanket together. "Don't worry, Jack. You'll always be my first porch companion. But you'll have to share me and the blanket with Clint now."

A puff of a huff and a contented purr was the cat's response.

As they walked back to the cabin, Clint wrapped an arm around Georgia's shoulders. "I'll try not to steal your blanket. Or your cat."

Georgia grinned. "Good. Because I think Captain Jack would win that fight."

Clint's cell phone chimed, the trill echoing through the quiet evening air. His eyes widened as he glanced at the glowing screen. "I can't believe it," he whispered, his voice rough with disbelief.

Her breath caught as she leaned in close. "What's happening?"

Clint turned the phone toward her, the screen illuminating both their faces with a bluish glow in the dusk. "It's Pops and Janis."

## *Chapter 20*

**T**he message from Clint's granddad and Georgia's grandmother was short, almost impossible to believe. *We're married!*

Georgia stared in stunned silence, her mouth open, unable to form words as Clint's phone glowed between them.

He let out a shaky laugh. "They just went. Didn't tell a soul. Pops and Janis flew to Hawaii and got married on the beach." Clint stared again at his phone. "Looks like the message was sent to a group. You might check your cell."

She ran to get hers. Sure enough, the message waited in her text inbox, followed by a photo of Pops in a Hawaiian shirt, Janis in a simple sundress and sunhat, both smiling as they stood hugging beneath a palm tree on the beach.

Georgia pressed a hand to her heart, tears threatening as she looked from the photo to Clint. "I can't believe it. Grandmother always said she wanted to see the world, but I never thought she'd do this."

"Guess they got their second chance."

"I can't believe they did that." She smiled through her tears, imagining them walking hand-in-hand on warm Hawaiian sand.

Clint rubbed the back of his neck. "I wonder where they'll live."

"Not sure. I guess we'll find out whenever they come back to town."

Georgia and Clint's cell phones both chimed with incoming texts. She glanced at the avalanche of messages from her mom, dad, aunts, and uncles. The family was in an uproar. Her parents were shocked but thrilled. Extended family members wanted further details and questioned Grandmother's sanity.

Clint let out a groan as he scrolled through his phone messages. "Looks like my family is going nuts."

Georgia sighed a happy sigh. "As surprised as I am about what they did, I think it's wild, unexpected, and utterly perfect."

He sent her a questioning look. "You like that they just up and got married?"

"Why not? They're adults, and I have no doubt they love one another."

"Yeah, I guess." Clint kept staring at his phone, a frown creasing his brow. "Would you do something like that?"

"Elope?" Georgia sputtered, wondering if his question was more than about their grandparents. "I ... I'm not sure."

His gaze jerked to her face. For a quick moment, he looked stunned, like he hadn't meant to ask that question about her. Then, a slight smile played on his lips. "Good to know." He turned his attention back to his phone.

The thought of Clint's intriguing question made her head spin, and a wave of giddiness washed over her. Not that she really wanted to elope. She'd prefer a lovely church wedding in the old stone church overlooking the Smoky Mountains. She'd wear a simple, but elegant dress, and stand next to Clint as they said their vows as family and friends watched from the old wooden pews. Then they would fly off to some wonderful destination before starting their lives together.

Not that she'd thought about that scenario that much.

Clint slid his cell into his back jeans. "I'd better let you get to sleep."

"As though I'm going to get any rest after that announcement. I've never been to Hawaii, have you?"

"Yeah, went once for a business conference. After the

meetings, the company shuttled us around in a small bus for a quick tour. It's beautiful, but seeing it from a bus window wasn't the way I'd want to enjoy the island." Clint took her in his arms. "Would you ever want to travel to Hawaii?"

Georgia nestled against him. "Visit Pearl Harbor and the USS Arizona Memorial, hike Diamond Head, and snorkel in Hanauma Bay. Lie on a tropical beach under palm trees, and swim in the ocean? I really haven't thought that much about it."

Clint chuckled. "Maybe someday you'll be able to go."

The following morning, Georgia stood beside her mother in Shaffer's Outfitters.

Her mother shook her head, a bemused smile playing on her lips. "I still can't believe Mom went and eloped. After all these years, after everything she used to say about tradition."

Georgia grinned. "Honestly, I think it's amazing."

Her mother pulled out her phone, scrolling to a blurry but joyful selfie of Janis and Wayne in front of a courthouse. "She texted this last night. Says she's never been happier."

Georgia studied the photo. "They look so in love."

"We're happy for them. It's just unexpected, that's all. And just maybe, it's a reminder that love doesn't always follow the rules."

Georgia wasn't sure what that statement meant. Was she supposed to be open to something less traditional if Clint ever proposed? And why would her mom even think like that? Did her mom know something? Was Clint going to actually propose? What would he have in mind?

Good grief. Georgia shook off her thoughts. She was overthinking. Obviously, she needed her morning sustenance to kick her brain into gear before she started work or allowed her thoughts to run even more rampant.

After checking with her mom about any needed supplies, Georgia made her way to the soda fountain.

Grinning, Melba slid Georgia's usual root beer float across the linoleum surface. "I saw you coming."

"Thanks!" Georgia held the cold glass in her hand, its frothy top crowned with a swirl of vanilla ice cream.

"I need to talk to you about something." Melba leaned in, lowering her voice to a conspiratorial whisper. "We want to hire you."

Georgia paused mid-sip, the icy sweetness lingering on her tongue. "We?"

Melba nodded, her eyes darting around the store, as if watching for eavesdroppers. "Me and Beatrice."

A wave of shock fluttered through Georgia as her eyebrows flew up. "You're talking to one another without wanting to pull one another's hair out?"

Melba bit her lip and nodded. "I know it's weird, but we talked the other night. Really talked and discovered things we didn't know about one another and about Harold. We decided to set aside our rivalry and find out what really happened to him."

"Your long-lost love?"

"Yep. We want to hire you to find the man, or at least find out what happened to him." Melba's hands, a little shaky, reached under the counter and lifted a bundle wrapped in faded tissue paper. "We've got photos, newspaper clippings, and a few envelopes from letters he sent us." Melba's cheeks reddened. "We wanted you to see the address, but not what was inside."

Georgia gave her a reassuring smile. "I'll do my best. And I'm proud of you both for putting aside your differences."

"Well, it was about time. We're not getting any younger, and I'm tired of being angry. We even forgave one another."

"Wow, this is a big deal. That's wonderful. You know, you even look different. Younger. More relaxed."

Melba took a deep breath and smiled. "I slept better than I have in years."

Georgia patted the bundle Melba had given her. "I'll take good care of what you shared."

"Thanks, sweet pea. Hopefully, you'll find out something positive, like Harold lost his memory and didn't just leave us in the dust."

"I'm sure there'll be a satisfactory answer for his disappearance."

"Hope so, for his sake. Beatrice and I forgave one another, not sure about Harold until we know the truth."

Chuckling, Georgia finished her drink and hurried back to her office. She had a Harold to find.

# *Chapter 21*

Georgia sat at her office desk with her head resting in her hands, daydreaming about Clint. Since they said they loved one another, their nightly parting was becoming increasingly difficult.

Pops and Janis were living in her grandmother's house, and their happiness and giggly laughter were like infatuated teenagers.

With a happy sigh, Georgia got back to work. After searching through old town records, the internet, social media, and the Veterans Administration, she'd finally found Harold.

She placed a call to the general store and told Melba the news. With an excited gasp, Melba promised to contact Beatrice.

Clutching her papers, Georgia bounced down the creaking wooden stairs. A few customers meandered through the store aisles.

Behind the counter, her parents, Pops, and Janis huddled close, their whispers and muffled laughter swirling in the air.

Georgia strode over. "Hey, what's going on?"

Four faces snapped up, their eyes wide.

Her dad darted away, busying himself with a customer inspecting the fishing rods.

"Hi, honey," her mom said in a sweet, soft voice as though they weren't up to something.

The others nodded, and Georgia eyed them suspiciously. "What were you talking about?"

"Stuff," Pops replied, his shoulders lifting in a careless shrug.

"Yeah," Janis agreed as she put her arm around her husband.

"Okay," Georgia said. "Well, I'm off to the General Store. Do ya'll need anything?"

"Nope. We're fine," her mom replied.

The rest nodded, a chorus of not-so-innocent grins.

Georgia shook her head. With a family like this, life was anything but boring.

A few minutes later, Georgia set the bundle the ladies had given her on the counter as she stood between Melba and Beatrice at the soda fountain. "I found him. While in the army, Harold served overseas. He then moved to Huntsville, where he worked in the space industry. He married, had kids and grandkids, and he's living there now."

Melba's eyes misted. "He always dreamed big. Probably helped put rockets on the moon."

"Looks like he did okay." Beatrice nodded.

Georgia showed them a recent photo of a silver-haired man smiling with his grandchildren. "Harold lost his wife two years ago."

Beatrice's gaze shot up. "He's single?"

Melba growled and grabbed Harold's photo. "Don't you get any ideas, Beatrice Finklebine."

"Me? It looks like *you* are the one with ideas since you have Harold's picture in your grubby hands."

"Grubby? How dare you? I'll have you know these hands are the cleanest of anyone in the county."

Georgia let out a loud whistle. "Wait a minute! What happened to your truce? Didn't you forgive one another? I thought you were friends again."

Melba hung her head and gave Beatrice a sheepish expression. "I'm sorry."

Beatrice's shoulders slumped. "I'm sorry too. I think it's time we moved on."

Melba set the photo on top of the bundle containing the newspaper clippings, photos, and envelopes from letters Harold had sent to the women. "Your friendship is more important than Harold. He let us go. Let's let him go." She picked up the bundle. "How about we go out back and have a burn party?"

"I'd like that, sweet friend."

The two women hugged, picked up the bundle, and walked arm in arm out the door.

"Hey, private-eye lady." Clint, his handsome self, dressed in jeans, a denim shirt, and a sheepskin coat, walked toward her. "Looks like you've solved a case that has haunted Garden Valley for decades and finally ended the feud for good. May I take you out this evening to celebrate?"

"Why, thank you, kind sir. I would be honored."

A grin spread across his face as he leaned down, his breath warm against her ear. "Wear something nice because I'm taking you to the new steakhouse. Can you be ready by six?"

"Yes, that sounds wonderful. I'll be ready." Georgia watched as he sauntered out like he was some cowboy rancher type. Which, if she thought about it, he was a rancher. A hot date with a rancher. What could get better than that?

Georgia hurried back to her office. She had to get a few more background checks done for companies before she could leave for the day.

She'd heard about the new steakhouse in town and couldn't wait to give it a try. Of course, if Clint had invited her to a food truck, she'd have been happy.

Thank goodness she had a flattering but still modest black

dress and a nice warm coat she could wear.

His nerves pinging all over the place, Clint checked his look in the mirror. Hopefully, Georgia would approve of his dress slacks, long-sleeve shirt, and nice loafers. He wanted to make a positive impression.

He picked up the velvet box from his dresser. Janis and Beth had advised him on which style of diamond to buy, and Pops and Richard had taken him to a jeweler they personally knew.

The princess-cut diamond sparkled in the gold band as he adjusted it in the light. Man, he hoped Georgia liked it, and he hoped she'd say yes when he proposed.

Clint wiped the sweat beading on his forehead. What if she said no? What if he was wrong about how she felt about him? His stomach clenched as a wave of nausea washed over him.

At least this time, he wouldn't have a crowd watching if she said no. Praying a desperate prayer for help and a positive outcome, Clint put the box in his pocket and headed out the door.

# *Chapter 22*

Clint checked his phone for the twenty-seventh time. He had thirty minutes left before he needed to pick up Georgia. The drive over would only take him ten to fifteen minutes.

He paced across the farmhouse den, his polished loafers making soft sounds against the hardwood floor. It still felt strange that the house and land were his now that Pops had moved in with Janis. Clint chuckled to himself, picturing two grown adults acting like love-struck teens, always sneaking kisses and holding hands. He wanted that now, a second chance at love, and he hoped this evening was the start of his own love story.

Clint stopped at the front picture window and glanced out at his spotless truck parked in the drive. His stomach dropped.

One back tire was completely flat, the rubber sagging, and the rim almost touching the ground. "No, not now."

He rushed outside, the brisk evening air biting his cheeks as he kneeled to inspect the damage. Dread pooled in his gut. There was no way he could change that tire and keep his slacks and shirt unmarred, not if he wanted to pick up Georgia on time.

What was he going to do? Clint pulled his phone from his back pocket and punched in Pop's number, and explained what happened.

"We're on the way," his granddad answered, the phone clicking as he ended the call.

Clint quickly glanced at the time again and then patted the

velvet box in his pocket. He sure hoped Pops would leave quickly so he could get him. He just had to get to Georgia on time.

Ten minutes later, Pops and Janis arrived, their car polished and gleaming in the late evening sun. Clint slid into the back seat, surprised by the sight of Pops and Janis, both in their best clothes and beaming like they shared a secret.

Clint stifled a groan. Is that why Pops had gotten here so fast, and Janis was with him? Had they planned to follow him and watch his proposal? He should never have shared his plan for the evening.

As they drove to Georgia's house, Janis and Pops kept chattering about the upcoming fall and Christmas fair, all while exchanging amused looks toward Clint.

When they arrived at Georgia's place, Clint leaped out of the car and sprinted to her front porch, barely making it with a minute to spare.

Georgia opened the door, and Clint's breath caught. The warm glow from the porch light haloed around her, accentuating how stunning she looked in the black dress, hugging her curves in all the right places. Her coat framed her shoulders, and as she smiled, Clint's nerves leaped even higher.

"Wow." Was all he could think of saying for a few seconds. "I mean, you look amazing."

A pink hue spread across Georgia's cheeks as she smiled. "Thank you. You look mighty fine and wow worthy yourself."

Clint threaded his fingers with hers and led her to the waiting car, where Pops and Janis looked at them all dreamy-eyed.

Georgia glanced at Clint and whispered. "I didn't know we were double-dating."

He offered her an apologetic look as he held open the car

door for her. "This wasn't part of the original plan. My truck had a flat, and the grandparents said they were already planning a date night."

"Either way, I'm looking forward to our evening together." Georgia slid into the seat and gazed at the older couple. "You two sure look nice."

Janis grinned over her shoulder. "What could be better than a special evening with the one you love?"

"I agree," Georgia smiled at Clint.

He nodded and smiled. Man, he wanted to kiss her, take her hand in his as he sat next to her. But his palms were sweaty, and he felt a touch nauseous as Pops gunned his car and drove toward town.

Garden Valley's new steakhouse buzzed with activity. The lights cast a soft glow over the polished wood tables, and the low murmur of conversations blended with gentle music.

The mouthwatering scents of perfectly seared beef, fresh herbs, and the faintest hint of roasted garlic made Clint's stomach rumble as he guided Georgia to their reserved spot.

His hand trembled slightly as he pulled out her chair. Trying to calm his hyperactive nerves, he settled across from her and spotted, three tables over, a pair of familiar figures: Georgia's parents, half-concealed behind their tall menus and peeking out every so often.

On top of that, Pops and Janis settled at a table too close for Clint's comfort since they were within earshot and observation range of their table.

The realization they were all here for this moment made his stomach twist tighter than a wedgie.

"This is so nice," Georgia said as she looked over the menu. "Way too nice to celebrate taking care of Melba and Beatrice's feud."

Clint grinned, grateful that he had an excuse to get Georgia here. "That was a big deal, you know?"

"Right." Georgia laughed softly. "Well, whatever the reason, thank you for bringing me here. It's fun to dress up and come somewhere nice."

Clint reached his hand out to take hers and instead knocked over his water glass. He jumped up and frantically grabbed a napkin to stop the spill from reaching Georgia.

She tried to help as a server, moving quickly with a white towel in hand, rushed to address the problem. Another server, a blur of motion reminiscent of a magician, whisked off the wet tablecloth, replaced it with a dry one, and in a matter of minutes, the table was reset.

Clint slumped back in his chair and swiped the perspiration from his forehead, sure that Georgia, her family, and everyone in the restaurant had witnessed his clumsiness.

"Are you okay?" Concern etched on her beautiful forehead, Georgia tilted her head, her eyes fixed on him as she studied him. "You seem nervous?"

"I'm fine." He pasted on his best smile, took a deep breath, and focused on the gorgeous woman across the table.

After the server took their order, Clint was still keyed up and wasn't sure how to start a conversation. Trying to focus, he found himself distracted by the constant chatter coming from the next table.

The woman's way-too-loud voice cut through the peaceful atmosphere. She barely seemed to pause for breath, her laughter and words ringing out, and yet somehow the woman's food mysteriously disappeared from her plate.

From Georgia's amused expression, she'd also noticed the woman.

Leaning in, Clint whispered to Georgia, "With all her talking, I don't know how she's ever taken a bite of her food, but it's still disappearing."

Georgia let out a light chuckle. "Maybe she's feeding by osmosis."

They shared a quiet laugh. Despite that, Clint found it nearly impossible to concentrate.

When the food arrived, despite the churning in his stomach, the aroma of the steak was too tempting to resist. As they ate, Clint asked what Georgia had found out about Harold and how it went with Melba and Beatrice. Fortunately, Georgia obliged with details that gave him time just to sit, eat, and enjoy her company.

He kept glancing toward the server, waiting to give the cue. Clint had called ahead and ordered a small, decadent chocolate cake. The pastry chef had agreed to write *Will you marry me* in delicate script across the glossy ganache.

Once they finished, the waiter cleared the table and gave Clint a quick nod. The time had finally come. He said another silent, desperate prayer heavenward that everything would go okay and she would say yes.

"I'll be right back," Georgia said as she rose to her feet. I need to powder my nose."

Clint wanted to grab her, tell her not to go. Not now. Out of the corner of his eye, he could see the waiter already walking toward them carrying the cake.

As soon as Georgia's back was to Clint, he motioned with his hand for him to stop.

The waiter's eyes widened, and a wave of pity washed over his features.

Clint groaned and hurried to where the man stood. "Wait a few minutes. She just went to the powder room."

"Oh, good." Relief crossed the man's features. 'Okay. I'll be back in a few."

Pops and Janis both gave nervous glances his way. Georgia's parents smiled and held up their hands in a praying position. Clint gave them a discreet nod. He could use all the prayers he could get.

After what felt like an eternity, but was likely just a few minutes, Georgia was back, sinking into her seat. "Are you ready to go?"

"Not yet. I ordered dessert."

"How sweet. No pun intended."

The beaming server made his way to the table, the cake raised in his hands. Clint's heart hammered in his chest as he discreetly pulled the velvet box out of his pocket and placed it in his palm.

With a flourish, the waiter presented the cake and placed it in front of Georgia.

Clint pushed back his chair and dropped to one knee beside her. Georgia's mouth dropped open, and her surprised, shining eyes rested on him. He flipped open the box, the princess-cut diamond sparkling under the lights.

All the nerves, the spectators, the noise faded away as he looked at the one he loved. "Georgia Shaffer, I love you. Will you marry me?"

Georgia's "Yes!" rang out, sweet and sure, drowning out any other sound.

He rose to his feet as she leaped up and threw herself into his arms.

The entire steakhouse seemed to pause, then erupt into applause, Pops and Janis beaming, Georgia's parents with delighted, tearful smiles, and Clint finally able to breathe.

# *Chapter 23*

The next morning, Georgia held her hand under her office desk lamp as she admired the sparkling diamond in the light. She still couldn't believe she was officially engaged. Oh my goodness, she was going to marry her teenage crush, Clint Briscoe!

Excitement had kept her awake most of the night as she scribbled down notes for the upcoming wedding. They hadn't set the date yet since she wanted to find out when the stone church in the mountains would be available.

Footsteps pounded on the stairs, and Tanya ran towards her. "I heard the news! You're engaged."

Georgia jumped to her feet, and the two danced around the room in celebration.

Tanya hugged her tight, then stepped back. "So, when's the big day?"

"Haven't set the date yet. I'm calling in a few minutes to find out when the stone church is available."

"When are you planning on picking out a dress?"

"Mom and Janis offered theirs, but I want one of my own. So, we're going shopping this weekend. Want to join us?"

"Yes! I'd love that. You get to say yes to the dress."

Georgia scrunched up her shoulders, the excitement almost too much to contain.

"Have you decided where you'll live?"

All those wonderful emotions crashed to the floor as she realized she didn't have a clue.

Georgia slumped back in her office chair. "Since Clint has a farm and cattle to watch over, he probably needs to be close to his property. But I don't want to leave my cabin behind."

"Wouldn't you rather be with Clint?" Tanya sat across from her.

"Yes, but it would be so strange living at his grandparent's farmhouse."

"It belongs to Clint now, and once you move in, you'll make it yours. And as for your cabin, you could keep an eye on it or rent it out to someone."

"Rent my family's cabin?" Georgia's stomach clenched at that thought. The place had been a family legacy for generations. "No one will take care of it like a family member." Then again, she couldn't imagine it sitting empty, unloved, and unattended.

"You never know. The town's expansion has created a housing demand. Maybe somebody would rent and look after the cabin for you."

"You don't think Clint would want to live there with me?"

"Clint would probably go wherever you want to live, but he has the farm to watch over. Besides that, the farmhouse on the property is really nice. I don't know why you wouldn't jump at the chance. Talk to your family about what they think should be done about the cabin. Even better, why don't you talk to God?"

Georgia glanced at her friend and sighed. "You're right. I'm overthinking and worrying instead of asking the right questions and praying. Too easy, you know?"

"Yep." Tanya chuckled. "We make life *so* much harder than it has to be. Let me know what I can do to help with the wedding plans. And one more thing, I know a wedding is a big thing, but don't forget to enjoy the journey."

"Thanks, friend. I'm going to call the stone church and find out their earliest date. Clint said he did *not* want a long engagement since we've known one another for years."

"I think that's wise. Keep me updated."

After Tanya left, Georgia placed the call and was surprised someone actually answered, and even more thrilled when she learned they had a date much earlier than she imagined, since someone had canceled. Georgia asked them to save the date and gave them the information and her credit card number to hold the church.

It was happening. Her wedding would be a few days before Christmas.

Georgia ended the call and hurried downstairs to find her mom and Janis chatting by the counter. "I got the church!"

Squeals of celebration filled the store.

"When's the date?" Her mom asked.

"December 20th," Georgia said with a big smile.

Georgia's mom and Janis both went wide-eyed.

"This December? That's too soon!" Her mom exclaimed. "You realize that's only a few weeks after Thanksgiving."

Her grandmother put a hand on her chest like she was going to faint. "How on earth will we be able to get everything done?"

"Why would that be a problem?" Georgia shrugged. "I don't want anything fancy. The church is available, so all I need to do is get a dress, make sure the minister is available, get a nice suit or tux for Clint, order a cake, find a reception place, and order flowers." With a long list still swirling in her mind, Georgia steadied herself against the cool, smooth counter. "Maybe we should elope."

"No!" Her mom wrapped Georgia in a hug. "We want to be there with you. We'll get it done."

Georgia gulped. "Oh, no. I've got to let Clint know. I hope his family can come."

Her mom scrunched up her nose. "That might be hard with the holidays so close and his brothers in the NFL and a firefighter."

"Ugh." Wringing her hands, Georgia paced back and forth. "What am I going to do? What if Clint wants to move it out further? Then again, he said he didn't want a long engagement."

Her mom took Georgia's hands in hers. "This is your wedding, between the two of you. It's about starting your life together. Don't let us or other family members ruin the timing of whatever you choose for your big day."

"Thanks, Mom." Georgia rushed back to her office and called Clint's mobile. He answered on the second ring, was thrilled with the early date, and promised to let his family know.

An hour later, he called Georgia back. His parents could come and were excited to meet her. The brothers weren't sure with their schedules, but promised they'd try to get there.

After the call ended, Georgia rubbed the birthmark on her chin. What if Clint's parents and brothers didn't like or approve of her? A bazillion insecurities attacked as she thought of all the things that could go wrong about the wedding and her relationship with Clint's family.

With a groan, she sank her head onto the desk and let out a whimper.

## *Chapter 24*

The warm glow of firelight danced, illuminating the room as they sat on her cabin couch, snuggled under a blanket. Georgia's tea, steaming and fragrant, warmed her hands while Clint sipped his coffee. Another perfect evening, and all the wedding plans were coming together as the last few weeks had passed in a blur.

Georgia had found her wedding dress at the second shop they visited, and it fit perfectly. No alterations needed. The minister was available on that date. Most of the town had shown up for their wedding shower, gifting them with a variety of items to start their married life together.

A wedding cake and flowers had been ordered, and Clint decided on a simple black tux. Pops would be his best man, and Tanya her matron of honor.

With the wedding just a week away, Georgia was still wrestling with her crazy insecurities. It was obvious Clint loved her, but what if his family didn't?

Georgia whimpered as she glanced at Clint. "What if your parents don't like me?"

Clint put his arm around her, pulling her close. "They will love you. It'll be fine. Hey, you said yes to my marriage proposal. My parents are thrilled I finally found someone who would actually marry me. Plus, we've had online visits with them, and everyone gets along great. You don't have to worry. You're a zillion times better than any other woman."

Georgia grinned as she glanced up at him. "A Zillion?"

Clint pressed his lips against hers with a long, sweet, and

slow kiss. "Yep. A zillion twenty times better."

She feigned a hurt expression. "I only went up twenty points? Well, let's see what I can do about that." She kissed him with passion, leaving them both breathless.

His deep chuckle reverberated in his chest. "Let me rephrase. I'll give you a zillion times a zillion times better."

Georgia grinned, "That's better because you are off any kissing chart."

After another kiss, Clint stood. "I'd better get home before we get in trouble. Captain Jack is probably prowling outside, waiting to pounce if I misbehave."

She rose to her feet and wrapped her arms around Clint. "I sure am looking forward to when we get to stay together."

"I sure am too." After another round of amazing kisses, he gave a heavy sigh and stepped out the door.

Georgia watched her fiancé drive away. In only a week, she'd be Mrs. Clint Briscoe. She hummed with happiness as she closed the door behind her and surveyed her cabin. She'd miss living here, but not enough to miss being full-time with Clint.

Right now, she needed to get her tail in gear and write more thank-you notes for the wedding gifts. Because soon she'd marry her best friend, fly off to Hawaii for a honeymoon, then move into Clint's farmhouse. No matter what happened, they would be together.

Four days later, Georgia tried not to fidget as she peered into the bakery's back room. The bakery employees were working and glancing her way with suspicious grins. The scent of vanilla and buttercream hung in the air, but the centerpiece of her dreams, the simple wedding cake adorned with sugar dogwoods, was supposedly nowhere to be found.

Clint, looking both amused and concerned, squeezed her

hand. "You sure you didn't order an invisible cake?"

She shot him a wry look. "Not helping, Mr. Briscoe."

Clint chuckled. "No worries, soon to be Mrs. Briscoe. We'll get it worked out."

Melba, acting as self-appointed wedding coordinator, bustled in, her clipboard clutched like a weapon. "I told you, I saw someone lurking around the bakery window last night."

Tanya burst through the door. "I've dusted for fingerprints. All I found was a trail of powdered sugar leading out the back."

Georgia tried to keep a serious expression, but couldn't stop her grin. "Very funny."

"We'll figure something out. Maybe we could order a bunch of sopapillas from Rosie's and stack them up like a wedding cake."

"Now that is a fun idea."

Georgia's grandmother rushed toward them. "I just checked the freezer. The only things in there are a bag of frozen peas and a note that says, 'If you want your cake, come to the gazebo at noon.'"

Clint's eyes widened. "A ransom note? For a cake?"

Georgia crossed her arms. "Ha, ha, ha. Why would there only be a bag of frozen peas in the bakery freezer and a ransom note? Someone is pulling my chain." She stepped toward the freezer.

Tanya pulled her back, stopping Georgia's progress. "We've checked. No need for you to look. It's almost noon. You'd better get to the gazebo."

"Okay, people, this is personal." Georgia tapped her foot. "Someone wants to sabotage our big day, or at least our dessert." Georgia headed for the door. "Clint, you're with me. Tanya, call for backup, preferably someone with a sweet tooth."

They hurried across the square, and Georgia squeezed

Clint's hand. "You ready for one last mystery before we tie the knot?"

He grinned. "With you? Always."

Georgia arrived at the gazebo and was taken aback by the sight of her parents, Pops and Janis, Oswald Chambers, Melba, Tanya, Blake, Mr. Grady, Beatrice, the police chief, and other townspeople, all beaming at her with broad smiles.

The police chief stepped forward. "Georgia Shaffer, before you get hitched, we wanted to thank you for the ways you've helped solve the many cases in our town, even at personal risk when lizards dropped from the sky." He chuckled but kept a straight face as he reached into a box. "So, as a token of our appreciation, we present you with the first Aloysius P. Higginbotham Sleuthing Award." He gave her a gleaming trophy with a golden hamster perched on top.

Georgia erupted in laughter as she received the prize. Glancing at her friends, she held it aloft. "Thank you, friends, family, noblemen, and noblewomen. I'm honored. I will do my best to continue to serve the town and make Aloysius P. Higginbotham proud."

The crowd roared with applause.

Clint smiled and leaned close. "I'm proud of you. And don't worry, the cake is safe. They just wanted to give you a fun adventure before the wedding."

Georgia couldn't stop laughing as her friends and family gathered around to congratulate her and wish her well.

# *Epilogue*

The scent of the ocean mingled with the warmth of the Hawaiian sun on her skin, Georgia relaxed in a beach chair beside Clint. The steady rhythm of the waves, like a soothing heartbeat, lulled Georgia into a dreamy state as she reminisced about their wedding day.

As her mind drifted, memories of their wedding day unfurled with vivid clarity. She could almost feel the crisp, cool air from that morning, tinged with the faint scent of pine that edged the path to the stone church perched high above the snow-dusted Smoky Mountains.

Georgia recalled the nervous swell in her chest dissolving the instant she met Clint's parents. His mother's kind eyes and the gentle squeeze on her hand, his father's booming laugh, and the warmth of their welcome enveloped her like a treasured quilt. Even Clint's brothers made her feel welcome and guided guests to their seats as they arrived.

During the ceremony, her gaze had clung to Clint, handsome and debonair in his crisp black tuxedo, his eyes shining and his lips stretched into a wide grin. As they pledged their vows, a shaft of sunlight streamed through the stained glass, casting rainbows across them as if God smiled on their marriage. Georgia sighed a silent prayer of thanks.

During the reception, the room echoed with laughter as guests shared stories and well-wishes. The only hitch came when Beatrice and Melba shamelessly flirted with Clint's brothers. The massive men seemed completely bewildered about how to respond to the older ladies' enthusiastic attention. Georgia smiled and couldn't wait to watch the video of their wedding and reception, since it all seemed to pass in a happy blur.

A delicate brush of lips on her shoulder pulled her from her reverie. Clint's grin was a flash of white against his tanned skin. "Never thought moving to Garden Valley would give me a second chance at love," he murmured, the husky timbre of his voice sending butterflies fluttering in Georgia's stomach, "especially with someone as famous as the winner of the coveted Aloysius P. Higginbotham Award."

She grinned at her handsome, amazing husband. Don't worry, I won't let it go to my head. No award will ever take your place." Georgia feathered her fingers along his soft, bearded face. "I've had a crush on you ever since we met, and I'm still crushing on you."

Clint chuckled. "I'm stunned and honored to be held in such high regard."

Sunlight danced across the water, blinding and golden, while the distant chatter of other beachgoers faded into the background as he stood and offered Georgia his hand.

He drew her close, wrapping her in a tight embrace, the feel of his strength making her feel safe and cherished. "Thank you, Mrs. Briscoe, for a perfect wedding and honeymoon. I hate to leave, but it's time to go home."

With one last lingering kiss, Georgia gathered her things. "I'm ready, Mr. Briscoe."

Hand in hand, their footprints pressed side by side in the sand as they dashed across the beach, and the promise of countless adventures yet to come.

# *The End*

# Thank you for reading

# *Clues, Crushes, and Second Chances*

# *Acknowledgments*

Heavenly Father, thank You especially for the tremendous gift of salvation You grant through Your Son, Jesus Christ. Thank You for Your help in times of need, and for providing comfort and healing to those who are hurting. Thank You for the sweet stories you have blessed me to write. May they bring honor and glory to Your name.

Dennis, thank you for being a loving, wonderful husband. Thank you for your prayers, support, and encouragement. I sure am grateful we are together.

Thank you, Patricia (Pacjac) Carroll, for your helpful feedback and for making the writing process so enjoyable.

JoAnn Durgin, thank you for creating another beautiful cover. You are a sweet blessing to me and so many others.

Readers, thank you for taking the time to read *Clues, Crushes, and Second Chances*. If you enjoyed the novel, would you be so kind as to leave a positive review and share the book with friends?

Please visit Lisa at https://lisabuffaloe.com
Facebook https://facebook.com/lisabuffaloe
Twitter (X) https://x.com/lisabuffaloe
Instagram https://instagram.com/buffaloelisa
Amazon https://amzn.to/4ltfEBA

# *About the Author*

Lisa Buffaloe is a happily married mom, speaker, and multi-published author. She loves spending time with God, her sweet hubby, studying the Bible, writing, and enjoying nature.

# *Books by Lisa*

## Fiction
Each book may be enjoyed separately or as part of the series.

### Garden Valley, TN Series
*Clues, Crushes, and Second Chances*

### Crawdad Beach Series

| | |
|---|---|
| *Visible, yet Hidden* | *Mia Lets Go* |
| *Running to Grace* | *A New Paige* |
| *Crystal's Journey Home* | *Running from Shame* |
| *A Baker's Heart* | *Elise's New Song* |
| *Stella's Heart Code* | *A Found Joy* |
| *River Steps Free* | *A Healing Rain* |

### Hope and Grace Series

| | |
|---|---|
| *Nadia's Hope* | *The Discovery Chapter* |
| *Prodigal Nights* | *Open Lens* |
| *Writing Her Heart* | |

## Stand-alone novels

*The Masterpiece Beneath*
*The Fortune*
*Grace for the Char-Baked*

## Non-Fiction

*Finding Freedom in a Binding World*
*Float by Faith*
*Heart and Soul Medication*
*Time with The Timeless One*
*The Forgotten Resting Place*
*Present in His Presence*
*We Were Meant for Paradise*
*One Lit Step: Devotions for your journey*
*The Unnamed Devotional*
*Flying on His Wings*
*Unfailing Treasures*
*No Wound Too Deep For The Deep Love of Christ*
*Living Joyfully Free Devotional (Volumes 1 & 2)*

# Clues, Crushes, and Second Chances

**Lisa Buffaloe**

www.ingramcontent.com/pod-product-compliance
Lightning Source LLC
Chambersburg PA
CBHW070335130626
46556CB00007B/2871